JEFFREY ROUND

BON TON ROULET

Jeffrey Round is an award-winning writer, director, filmmaker, publisher, essayist, and playwright who has encouraged the development of LGBT literature, particularly in Canada.

He is the Lambda-Award winning author of *Lake on the Mountain*, the first Dan Sharp mystery, as well as the acclaimed Bradford Fairfax mystery series. Twice nominated for a ReLit Award for poetry (*In the Museum of Leonardo da Vinci*) and fiction (*The Honey Locust*), he also penned the stand-alone mystery *Endgame*, dubbed a "punk rock reboot" of Agatha Christie's *And Then There Were None*. His first two books, *A Cage of Bones* and *The P-town Murders*, were listed on *AfterElton's Top 100 Greatest Gay Books*.

In 2002, his short film, *My Heart Belongs to Daddy*, premiered at the prestigious *Director's View Film Festival*. It won awards for Best Canadian Director and Best Use of Music at the *Hollywood North Movie Festival,* and the Schweppes Prize at what would become the first annual *Canadian Film Fest*. In 2005, Jeffrey was nominated for the *KM Hunter Artist Award for Literature* for "a body of work" that included fiction, poetry, drama, and literary criticism.

In 1991 he founded *The Church-Wellesley Review*, Canada's first journal for creative LGBTQ writing. In 2009, he founded *Proust and Company*, a musical and literary salon, and in 2015 he was a co-founder of *The Naked Heart Festival of Words*.

You can find him on Facebook, Blogspot (A Writer's Half-Life), Twitter (@BradfordK9) and at www.jeffreyround.com.

Acclaim for Jeffrey Round's

BRADFORD FAIRFAX MYSTERY SERIES

BY JEFFREY ROUND

The BRADFORD FAIRFAX *mystery series:*

The P-Town Murders
Death in Key West
Vanished in Vallarta
Bon Ton Roulet

The Lambda-winning DAN SHARP *mystery series:*

Lake On The Mountain
Pumpkin Eater
The Jade Butterfly
After the Horses
The God Game

Other books:

A Cage of Bones
The Honey Locust
Endgame

Poetry:

In the Museum of Leonardo da Vinci

BON TON ROULET

A Bradford Fairfax Murder Mystery

by Jeffrey Round

ROUNDER PUBLICATIONS

ROUNDER PUBLICATIONS, 2017

This book is a work of fiction. All characters, institutions
and public figures mentioned herein have been used
fictionally throughout. An statements or situations
ascribed to such are purely works of the imagination.

First published in 2017 by Rounder Publications
FIRST EDITION

www.rounderpublications.com

Round, Jeffrey
Bon Ton Roulet / Jeffrey Round
(The Bradford Fairfax Murder Mystery Series, vol. 4)
Issued in print and electronic formats.
ISBN: 978-09810606-4-4 (pbk)
ISBN 978-09810606-5-1 (ebook)

I. Title II. Series: Round, Jeffrey.
Bradford Fairfax murder mystery; vol. 4

Cover design: David Heath
Cover image: Frances "Fannie" Benjamin Johnston (PD)
House of the Turk, Dauphine Street, New Orleans, 1937-38
Back cover: Author's collection

For Greg Herren & Paul J Willis
and
Floyd McLamb & Stuart Anthony

What is life? Perhaps it is a riddle that does not have to be solved.

YUKIO MISHIMA, *Forbidden Colours*

BON TON ROULET

A Bradford Fairfax Murder Mystery

1

New Orleans was as unrepentant as a drunk come sunup on Sunday. A thunderstorm hovered in the distance, making the horizon dance with ghostly flashes while the sky glowed with a feverish hue. From nearby came the moan of the mighty Mississippi wending its way past Louisiana's shores.

Music swelled inside bars and shanties along the river's edge, spilling out onto the streets where the occasional reveller stumbled home in the pre-dawn darkness. Here and there, a stray dog howled to unsettle the night. After all, this was the Deep South where nearly everything sang the blues.

A bonfire burned brightly inside an abandoned warehouse, the flames stretching to the ceiling. Shadows flickered and grew, thrown high against the walls, as a tribe of scantily clad young men moved restlessly around the makeshift blaze. Bradford Fairfax, a.k.a. Agent Red, crouched just outside the circle of light and watched.

Brad counted twelve boys in total. Too many to

challenge directly, but that had never been his intention. From what he could see, the pack was comprised of every discernible race—black, white, Asian, Middle-Eastern, aboriginal—each one a superlative specimen of manhood, making for a gathering of the finest humanity had to offer. Or possibly finer than anything humanity had to offer.

Brad had been careful to enter the warehouse downwind. He knew to be wary of these boys. They felt things beyond the range of ordinary humans. It was as if they possessed a sixth sense that tickled their noses and prickled their skins.

Twenty feet ahead, a sentry leaned against a wall. The boy's head nodded downward to his chest until a harsh whistle unsettled him. He looked up then pushed off from the wall with a grunt, heading for the far end of the cavernous space.

Brad heard the first spattering of rain on the roof. He'd been waiting all night for this moment. Standing just outside the perimeter of light, he watched the sentry's retreating form. In the flickering shadows, the graffiti-covered walls gleamed with a day-glow collection of crude sayings and obscene drawings. Keeping an eye on the boys, Brad slipped behind a towering coil of rope. The pile felt rough and scratchy to his fingers as he leaned forward to get a better look.

It was here, four days earlier, that he last saw his partner, Zach. Since then, it had been a frantic time of waiting and hoping Zach would turn up with some strange but entirely plausible explanation for his absence. Watching this eerie gathering put a chill in Brad's heart. He'd seen these boys kill with the flick of a wrist. Who knew what they might have done to Zach? So far the police had been less than helpful, though that was no surprise. If he had to deal with one more surly, slow-talking New Orleans cop, he'd really blow his cool. To hell with the consequences.

He watched curiously as one of the muscular beauties padded softly to the centre of the warehouse. The boy bent down and snatched up a pair of sticks from the ground. Hefting them with a cry, he turned his attention to a battered trashcan, tossing the lid Frisbee-style across the open space. Another boy leapt up and caught it mid-air. The pair began to beat a tom-tom rhythm, thumping out a primitive riff on the can and lid. The sound filled the warehouse. From above, as if in answer, came the steady tap-tapping of the rain.

A third youth began an awkward soft-shoe shuffle in time to the rhythm. Others joined in with little yips and yelps of excitement, their skin glistening where the flames licked at their sweaty torsos. Brad wondered yet again where this strange band came from. New Orleans had always been half wild and prey to exotic rumours, starting with Voodoo queen Marie Laveau and her cult of darkness. Lately, it had been followed by the vampire blood lust of Anne Rice. It was a strange and colourful place. Always had been and likely always would be. Currently, it was overrun by a

3

tribe of spectacular young men living along the riverbank in warehouses deserted in the wake of Hurricane Katrina eight months earlier.

From the very beginning New Orleans was a city of outcasts. Founded by French Acadians expulsed from Lower Canada by the British in the early-1700s, they evolved into "Cajuns" along the way and in turn helped defeat the over-cocky Brits in the Battle of New Orleans a century later. The Cajuns were later joined by Haitian refugees, freed slaves, and self-made men and women of all races and languages, making New Orleans the most unique and colourful city in North America. Long before Provincetown or Key West, the eccentric had become everyday here and the city a place where almost anyone could belong. Anyone who wanted to, at least.

With its history of runaway slaves and freemen of colour, it was no coincidence that New Orleans was also the first city in North America to elect a black official. Along the way, it also gave birth to jazz, a genuine Voodoo queen, Mardi Gras, and—lest we forget—Mardi Gras's younger gayer cousin, Southern Decadence. America was still recovering from the shock of it all in the twenty-first century.

Since that fateful August when Katrina laid waste to the city, however, all rules of play were turned on their heads. No one knew for sure how many former residents had relocated elsewhere and how many had simply died in the storm and their bodies been lost. By the following spring, one thing was clear: the New Orleans of the past was gone and would never return.

While picking up the pieces of their lives in those devastating months after the hurricane, the remaining residents were faced with a choice. They could reconstruct their beloved town and make it a better place than before or they could turn down a road leading to something few wanted—a city for the elite, where no one got along. The scales already seemed to be tipping in favour of the latter. Recently, New Orleans had been proclaimed the murder capital of North America.

Just then another of the boy beauties ducked in under the arches, brushing the rain from his limbs and shaking it from his hair. If Brad hadn't known better, he might have thought them ordinary kids out for a bit of fun. But he knew better. There was a wildness that distinguished them from regular boys, as telling as the difference between dogs and wolves. At first glance they looked the same, but somehow they weren't the same. Whatever they were, Brad knew to stay as far away from them as possible. There was no way he was letting one of them get close, with their cool touch and faint blue colouring as though an ink stain had spread beneath their skin. Still, he was determined to do whatever it took to find Zach and free him from whoever was holding him prisoner. *Prisoner*. The word stung. But he knew Zach would have returned by now if he'd been in any way able to do so.

The drummers continued their frenzied

beating. Others had taken up the rhythm, clapping hands and shuffling feet. Sinewy muscles gleamed in the fire's glow, while eerie cries filled the air like the howl of dogs catching scent of prey. It had just begun to dawn on Brad what those sticks were: bones. And they were long enough to be of the human variety.

A drop of sweat rolled from Brad's brow and down his nose, clinging for a moment before falling. He reached out a hand to swipe it away, but missed. In slow motion, he watched the drop fall to the floor where it was absorbed by the dust.

That could be bad news. It was exactly the kind of thing these boys seemed to sniff out, as though they had some sort of built-in lust-o-metre marking the cravings of ordinary mortals. He feared what would happen if one of those prowling creatures caught his scent.

Just outside the ring of fire, a trapdoor led to some dark netherworld beneath the warehouse where ships once docked to offload their cargo. Since Katrina, however, none of the piers was operative. Every now and again, one of the boys descended briefly into the unseen cavern below, returning with an exultant cry.

Clearly, something was going on down there. Brad wondered if that was where they were keeping Zach. If Zach was even still alive, that is.

Over the past four days, Brad had diligently searched every single warehouse for clues as to where his partner had gone. Not surprisingly, the police had written off his claims of a roving gang of renegade killers as lunatic fringe or maybe just a wildly exaggerated description of the thousands of refugees currently living in tents beneath overpasses or in derelict buildings.

To the NOLA cops, another random disappearance wasn't exactly news and with the soaring crime rate they already had plenty to keep them occupied. Moreover, Brad had no proof of his lover's disappearance in an area heavily marked *No Trespassing*. Nor was he at liberty to explain that he and Zach were actually secret agents working for a nameless security organization that recognized no official government body. Even if he had, that organization, known simply as Box 77 after its post office number, would have disavowed all knowledge of their existence, as well as its own. As far as the world was concerned, Box 77 didn't exist, so it was no surprise the police had fixated more on what two gay tourists were doing at an abandoned warehouse in the dead of night rather than the fact that Zach had disappeared while Brad lay unconscious after being attacked by persons unknown.

During the first few days of his search, Brad found nothing. It wasn't until the fourth day that he came across the same tribe of boys he'd seen the night Zach disappeared. He followed their wild romp along the coastline, past the dark eddies of the Mississippi and down into the heart of the warehouse district. Eventually, they'd led him right back here, where he'd been knocked on the head by an unseen assailant the last time he'd seen

Zach alive.

As Brad peered from behind the coiled rope, the whoops and cries grew louder, the tribe's antics more frenzied. It seemed like the prelude to something, but he couldn't tell what. Nothing about these boys made much sense. All he knew was that they were to be feared.

The rain continued to beat a tattoo on the tin roof. Brad crouched in the shadows, waiting for a sign. It could come at any time and he needed to be ready.

Just then the trapdoor lifted and a figure began to emerge. A frenzy erupted. The boys let out a collective howl, as though greeting a long lost friend. It seemed to Brad as if he were witnessing some sort of initiation ceremony. And this would be the new initiate, he told himself.

The trapdoor fell back with a resounding thud. The new boy stood before them wearing a plain tracksuit. His body was lithe and muscular, with a hoodie covering his head and obscuring his face. Apart from being slightly overdressed compared to the rest of the crowd, he seemed much like the others, another exquisite specimen of manhood.

A sharp *crack!* resounded from the parking lot, followed quickly by a second. This was the sign Brad had been waiting for. Now it begins, he thought. He hoped Harlan was already far away.

The boys stopped dancing and focused their attention on the sounds coming from outside. Almost as one, they set off for the parking lot. All but the new figure, who seemed unaware of what was going on. Eventually, he too began to follow the others, but his footsteps were slow and unsteady, a tagalong kid trying to keep up with his older brothers.

Once the boy in the hoodie was out of sight, Brad dashed to the trapdoor and tugged on the latch. It was heavy, but finally yielded to his effort. A set of uneven wooden stairs descended to a dank, narrow corridor beneath the warehouse. River stench permeated the air. From the other side of the wall came the rumble of rushing water. Brad pulled out his penlight and followed the passage to a metal door.

It opened at his touch.

Inside, the walls of the chamber gleamed blue-white. Brad glanced over a bewildering array of tables and machines outfitted with blinking lights. At first sight, it appeared to be a mortuary. Certainly some kind of scientific or medical work seemed to have been performed here, but what exactly went on was impossible to guess.

He skirted the room, searching for hidden doors or access routes that might possibly conceal a human being. A set of watery footprints led from a standing metal cabinet and trailed directly across the floor. Curious, Brad opened the cabinet and peered in at what looked like a make-shift shower. Multiple shower heads dangled overhead, while tangled on the floor lay something like the discarded skin of a very large snake. There was nothing else. Whatever the cabinet might once have held, Zach wasn't here now, if he ever had been.

Brad made his way back upstairs, closing the trapdoor behind him. The bonfire burned quietly at the centre of the warehouse, while outside the fireworks continued to explode. The smell of cordite drifted in through the open doors, along with the startled yips and yelps of the tribe. As Brad slipped back into the shadows he heard the slither of footsteps gliding over a slippery surface followed by a heavy grunting, as though something massive were being lifted with sheer brute force.

In the darkness, he could make out the towering coil of rope toppling toward him. He leapt aside as it landed with a thud, reverberating through the warehouse. A flare from the bonfire showed Brad he wasn't alone. The boy in the hoodie had returned. And while he may have been slow moving, he was certainly strong. Strong enough to topple a massive cog-wheel.

The two stood facing one another in the dark, each listening to the quiet breathing of the other. Brad wondered what to do. These boys were formidable. The prospect of hand-to-hand combat with one of them offered what would almost inevitably be a losing proposition.

There was no time to think, however. The boy let out a sudden howl. Whether it was a battle cry or a signal to alert the others didn't matter, because there was no way it wouldn't have been heard. The boy approached warily, like an animal circling its prey. His pupils gleamed in the darkness.

A metal hook dangled overhead. Brad's eyes followed the rope to its trajectory. The pulley was intact. If he could reach it, he might be able to climb up to the rafters. Then what? The place would soon be swarming with these diabolical monkeys. He couldn't stay up there forever. The climbing quadrupeds would eventually get to him.

Before Brad could decide, the boy lunged. Clammy hands gripped his throat. Instinctively Brad reached up, smashing the hook into his attacker's skull. An inhuman sound pierced the air as the hold relaxed. The boy went limp and fell to the floor. Bradford stepped back and waited. The body twitched for five, ten, fifteen seconds, before it finally stopped and lay there unmoving.

He knelt and put a finger to the boy's jugular. No pulse. The neck was broken. He hadn't intended to kill the boy, but if he hadn't connected the first time it would have been Brad who was lying there dead right now.

"I'm sorry, pal, but it was you or me," he said, pulling the hoodie from the boy's head.

Blue hair tumbled from beneath the garment. Brad cried out as he stared down at Zach's lifeless face.

2

As the plane dipped and headed for the runway at Louis Armstrong International Airport, Zach craned his head to catch a glimpse of the city. Brad gave his blue-haired lover an indulgent smile. *N'Orleans*, as the natives called her, was one of the most unique cities in the US. Or the entire world, for that matter. Its heritage stretched back hundreds of years and across many cultures. Katrina had merely been the latest in a series of events, some good and some bad, that marked its history and set it apart from so many other places.

Brad was anxious to see for himself what shape the city was in. It wasn't exactly an optimal time for a visit, with the disaster so recent. The world had watched in admiration tinged with disbelief as the former-residents returned to pick up their lives in whatever way they could. Predictably, many were asking what drove the survivors to return to a place that had been all but wiped from the map. Only a native N'Orleaner could say for sure, but even if it was just the urge to go where the weather suited your clothes, one thing was certain: the pull was strong.

In the weeks immediately following Katrina's catastrophic landfall, government aid had been intolerably slow to reach those living in the city's drowned corpse. For a while it seemed as though they might lose New Orleans forever. But the pumps had finally been repaired and the levees rebuilt. And now the residents were coming home again.

Looking down over the city, they saw a patchwork quilt of shingles and bright blue canvases—FEMA's temporary tarpaulin covers—dotting the rooftops below. In the distance, gaunt-looking high-rises glinted in the midday sun, standing gap toothed where the storm had taken out most of their windows. Brad pointed to the massive eggshell of the Louisiana Superdome. Nestled at the heart of the city, it had played a dominant part of the recent drama.

"That's where thirty thousand desperate people slept and ate while waiting for the disaster recovery teams to declare the city ready for habitation again," Brad said. "It was a living hell for the survivors, by the sounds of it."

A minute later, the plane shuddered as its wheels touched down. The new arrivals debarked and collected their bags, stowing them in the back of a cab. The trail of destruction was clearly evident as they headed along the highway. Watermarks stained causeway girders and the sides of buildings. Worse was still to come when they reached the city proper, especially in the outlying parishes. Many of the neighbourhoods were already permanently below sea level, having survived this long thanks only to the levees that Katrina's awesome forces finally destroyed.

As they reached the famed French Quarter, however, Brad was hard put to see signs of damage. The historic centre had largely been spared. Yes, here was the New Orleans he knew and loved, barely changed, despite everything it had been through. The bars and pubs along Bourbon Street resounded with a living pulse of sound as tourists once again thronged the streets. Even the streetwalkers still strutted just as outrageously, if a trifle more sombrely than they once did.

The heart of the city, it seemed, had been spared. That at least was a sliver of good news among all the bad. Here was the New Orleans of legend. The bride had been stripped bare, but she was still vibrant and alive. Though many loved her, she was by no means a beautiful woman. Nor was she good. She was a slut, a whore, a slattern, while the French Quarter was a blousy old tart with a voice like a strangled crow and a permanent case of the blues. But nobody minded. Nobody who mattered, anyway.

Brad and Zach watched in fascination as the cab zipped along to the Faubourg Marigny, where they would be staying at a small but discreet guesthouse that suited their purposes. The Lion's Roar was in fact a high-tech stronghold equipped with the latest technological marvels under the guise of an ordinary B&B. The owners, a younger/older British-American couple, had been shanghaied by Box 77 to assist in a covert operation some years earlier after accidentally stumbling on an agent's secret identity. Having acquired a taste for intrigue, the couple offered their modest little B&B as a potential Safe House. While it wasn't officially employed by Box 77, the Lion's Roar was definitely on its list of hidden assets. It had served the organization well on several occasions, which was why Brad and Zach had chosen it as their home base for the current assignment.

Brad had been with the organization for a while, working for a mysterious, smoky-voiced woman named Grace after having been wooed to join her agency some years earlier. Now it was Zach's turn. He'd become a full-fledged agent earlier that year. Following the gruelling initiation that all potential agents were subjected to, Zach graduated with flying colours to no one's surprise.

The blue-haired newcomer had also impressed a few hardened old-timers with his display of mental pyrotechnics known as "Remote Viewing" by CIA operatives who had practiced similar feats in the dark days before the dismantling of the Cold War. Zach, however, had not picked up his techniques in North America but rather in Tibet under the tutelage of Buddhist monks. When asked about his abilities, he would insist it was a skill, not a talent.

"Anybody can learn it," he said of his abilities. "Given a year of your undivided attention and your willingness to practice the exercises diligently, I can teach anyone."

Heady words, indeed. According to highly

classified CIA documents, one of their best practitioners had been renowned for being able to stop the heart of a goat simply by staring at it in mute concentration. Zach, however, was not into "party tricks," as he dubbed them. On the other hand, he astounded his superiors by describing the contents of sealed envelopes, sight unseen, in addition to informing his examiners of their mental and emotional states with unyielding accuracy as they plied him with questions.

"You need to learn to forgive," he told one startled questioner. "Hanging onto all that anger is giving you indigestion. Eventually, it will give you a heart attack." To another, he said, "Your wife just left you, but don't worry. You're about to meet the love of your life." "Really? What's her name?' asked the man, after confirming that he and his wife had just separated. "Fred," came the reply.

"Okay, so you can do some fancy stuff. But where does the information come from?" Brad insisted, being logic minded.

Zach cocked an eyebrow at him. "The Akashic Records. Otherwise known as the Library of Universal Knowledge, which is located somewhere on the etheric plane. Good luck trying to locate it, though. I don't think it has a postal address."

And so New Orleans was set to become Zach's first official assignment as the newly conscripted Agent Kong. He was looking forward to working alongside his partner, Agent Red, though Brad had misgivings about this. Still, Grace had put the pair together, having complete faith in her top agent and her top new recruit. Together they would perform wonders, she proclaimed.

So far, from what they could make of their assignment, Grace expected them to be on the lookout for unusual activities centred around New Orleans's highly contentious reconstruction process. She'd issued this edict somewhat obliquely over the phone before their departure.

"'Unusual' as in 'graft'?" Brad asked. "'Unusual' as in how the city has become the murder capital of the country?"

"Sure," Grace replied. "All that and more. Just keep your eyes open. I'm told they even have a Voodoo queen down there, so keep a close watch over your shoulders, too."

It was certainly a vague answer, Brad noted. Which meant that no one at the agency was talking openly at this point. Grace also asked them to keep their ears open for anything they might hear concerning the Federal Emergency Management Agency's response to the disaster. "Irregularities" with FEMA were said to "abound." Whatever that meant.

What it meant as far as Bradford Fairfax was concerned was that he was on another catch-as-catch-can operation. Meaning fly by the seat of your pants. Meaning go in and get the goods without really knowing what the goods are. It was going to be *that* sort of operation. One of Grace's specials. And Bradford Fairfax a.k.a. Agent Red was Grace's favourite candidate for just that sort of job. Now, tellingly, she'd added Zachary Tyler, newly christened Agent Kong, to the roster.

And so they found themselves stepping from a

17

cab on Chartres Street in the Faubourg Marigny, a district that lay south-east of its more famous cousin. Not quite as commanding as the French Quarter, Brad referred to the Faubourg Marigny as Funkytown. With its two- and three-tone Easter-egg coloured houses, the Marigny was about as Anything Goes as it got. Brad loved every inch of this not-quite-seedy, not-quite-upscale district where you could find yourself rubbing shoulders with just about any sort of person on any given day.

Bradford glanced up at the dreamy façade of the Lion's Roar. Behind a rustic iron grill the inn's two feline namesakes poised mid-roar, menacing arriving visitors from the other side of the gate. Brad pressed the buzzer. In seconds, a youthful, highly-energetic man in his mid-60s bounded down the walk, hailing them loudly as he shooed away a plethora of dogs whose job it seemed to be to greet guests as loudly and emphatically as possible.

"Miss Muffet! Mr. Tuffet! Get back inside," he cried. "Lola Girl and Digger Dog, you too! Git, y'all."

The dogs obeyed reluctantly as the gate clicked open.

"You lovely boy! It's been far too long!" Philip exclaimed, kissing Brad on both cheeks. "The world has turned and the city has mourned, but here y'all are again, and ah must say it is an honour to have you back with us, and please excuse the mess because we all are in the midst of renovations due to that nasty you-know-what of

18

which we do not speak."

The effusive Philip was the Southern half of the inn's partnership. The other half consisted of the demure and boyishly handsome Derek, a UK refugee-cum-war-bride who had stopped his roaming when he hit the shores of Lake Pontchartrain and promptly fell in love with Philip, nearly three decades his senior.

"Philip Grainger ... Zachary Tyler," Brad introduced them.

"Zachary? Why, ah do declare that is a Southern name. Y'all must be kin. Let me deliver a big N'Orleans welcome to you," Philip said, handily hugging Zach and nearly lifting him off the ground as he delivered a loud kiss to each cheek. "Y'all are just a livin' doll!"

Zach beamed as he was set back on the ground.

Philip turned to Brad. "My compliments. You, sir, are obviously an admirer of younger men, like me. And y'all have found yourself one gem of a youngster."

"And far wiser than his years might suggest," Brad said.

"C'mon, darlings. Derek's got the room all set up for you," Philip said, relieving them of their bags before they could protest. "He is *so* looking forward to having you both here!"

And with that he bustled down the laneway to the back of the property, a raucous combination of southern charm and congeniality, chatting over his shoulder at them the entire time.

"How has it been?" Brad called out, trying to keep up with the older man. "I imagine the tourist industry is still down since the troubles."

"Not good at all," Philip called out. "But we are making the best of it. What else can a body do?" He paused, suitcases in hand, to consider the courtyard. "Right now, the place is pretty well empty except for a cute little Japanese couple. Male, of course, and newly married. Ah gather this is a bit of a honeymoon for them. Apparently they're beekeepers or some such. From what ah understand, and that may be none too much, it seems they're here trying to find some special kind of bees for a film they're making. Ah think they're documentarians or something like that. Other than that, y'all'll mostly have the place to yourselves." They had reached the back of the inn. "Oh! Except for a sweet little ole gurrl," he exclaimed, managing to make the word sound both a mystery and a menace.

"A girl?" Brad asked.

"Yes," Philip rejoined, eyebrows raised. "A real one!"

Without another word—by all accounts an unusual feat for him—Philip directed them to a small cabin adjacent to the main inn. He set their bags on the floor and turned with a smile.

"It's *so* exciting whenever Bradford shows up," he told Zach. "But don't let me keep y'all. Derek is always after me not to talk the new arrivals to death and ah told him under no circumstances would ah do such a thing and he knows that ah am good for my word. 'Honey,' ah said, 'y'all know ah am a kind and considerate host', but if ah don't greet the guests and tell them everything ah know about the city when they arrive, why ah would feel ah hadn't done my duties as a—!"

Their excitable host clapped two fingers over his lips. "Hush my mouth. Ah am gone."

He gave them each another hug and repeated his rejoinder that Derek was looking forward to seeing them. Then, with traces of Southern gallantry, he tweaked their cheeks and left them to recover in the wake of his own mini-Katrina.

Brad looked at Zach and smiled. "That's Philip."

"Nice to be appreciated," Zach said.

"He was so excited he forget to comment on your hair," Brad said.

They had just started to unpack when Philip knocked and re-entered without waiting to be asked in.

"Blue hair!" he cried. "Ya'll have blue hair. Will wonders never cease?"

And with that, the whirlwind was gone once again.

The grounds of the Lion's Roar boasted a compact swimming pool, a hot tub, a well-stocked goldfish pond, and a garden filled with fragrant flowers and towering palms extending right to the back of the property. To Zach's surprise, Brad shook his head at the suggestion of a dip in the pool and bypassed the hot tub altogether.

"Something else takes precedence at the moment," he said, his eyes aglow. "What I like to do first when I arrive in New Orleans is to celebrate southern-style!"

"Does that mean you're going to take off all

21

your clothes and dance naked in the streets?" Zach asked.

Brad's eyes narrowed suspiciously. "Did I tell you about the time I got drunk at Southern Decadence?"

"No, not that I can recall. But now you'll have to tell me." Zach beamed. "So, what is the first thing you do?"

Brad's eyebrows rose in anticipation. "Have a mint julep!" he cried. "Nothing says 'Southern' like a mint julep."

They walked the few blocks to the Country Club, a palatial resort where Brad had stayed in his younger years before joining Box 77. Back then his cool northern demeanour had gone against the grain of the city's wild abandon. It had taken some time to be accepted by the others, but he eventually succeeded in joining in the fun.

They strolled through the high-ceilinged lobby, its gilt-framed doorways and potted ferns redolent of southern plantations and all-night jazz parties during prohibition. Turning down a long hallway, they headed into the bar where a dashing waiter made a beeline for them. Brad ordered a mint julep for himself and a mojito for Zach.

"Better start slow," he advised.

"What's the difference between them?" Zach asked, reclining in a wicker chair under a slow-moving ceiling fan.

"A mojito is made with white rum and cane sugar," Brad explained. "It's relatively safe. A mint julep, on the other hand, is made with bourbon and soda. Bourbon is far deadlier than most people realize. It's even worse than tequila. It almost proved my undoing on my first trip to New Orleans. You're not much of a drinker, so you're probably too unschooled for bourbon, but you can have a sip of mine if you promise to let me take advantage of you later."

Zach grinned. "You can take advantage of me now, if you like. Right here in the bar. I won't protest."

Brad harrumphed. "And that is precisely why you shouldn't have a julep just yet. I was exactly your age when I first tried one. Let's just say they do terrible things to a young man's willpower."

He still vividly recalled a particular night at the Country Club more than a decade ago. He'd been in his early twenties then. Despite his willingness to indulge, Southern Decadence had proved a dismal failure to his sensual proclivities. Bourbon changed all that. One hot sultry evening while hoping for an amorous encounter, Brad joined a smattering of guests poolside at the back of the resort. Three mint juleps to the wind, he suddenly lost his chilly northern reserve. Not only did he relate his entire life story to a crowd of perfect strangers, he also spent the latter half of the party lying on the bar, looking up at the stars, while those same perfect strangers slurped round after round of bar shots poured into his navel as Brad giggled and squirmed in delight.

Some hours later, he woke to find himself still lying there, the stars having shifted considerably, with dawn about to break and the party long since dispersed. To his surprise, apart from his sticky,

23

liqueur-stained torso, which had undergone a very thorough licking, he was still clothed. He dimly remembered tearing off his T-shirt and using it to clothe an inflatable duck in the pool, claiming it had complained of being cold. Amazingly, however, Brad's slip-on shorts remained intact. It was a wonder no one had taken advantage of him back in the days when he'd been considered fall-down-dead gorgeous, even with his red-tinted hair. But southern graciousness and good manners had prevailed, it seemed, precluding the other guests' taking advantage of an innocent, half-naked boy, even in New Orleans. Sometimes, Brad thought, there was a downside to being *too* well mannered.

Now, with Zach at his side, the afternoon passed in a flurry of alcohol and nostalgic recollections. After his first julep, Brad's accent lost its crisp northern exactness, slipping into something a bit more relaxed and Mason-Dixon Line-ish. After his second drink, his smile seemed on the verge of sliding to the other side of his face. It was late afternoon by the time the pair returned to the Lion's Roar, one thoroughly upright and the other slightly tipsy.

The patio, deserted when they left, was now occupied by a solitary figure. She sat staring off across the pool with a gaze so distant she might have been looking across an ocean. Soft breezes toyed with the hem and sleeves of a yellow sundress. Her Katherine Hepburn profile and up-swept hair suggested a line of strong, resilient women from half a century earlier. Bright eyes

24

offset a gloomy expression as she sipped from a half-finished glass before setting it on the tabletop.

"The 'gurrl,'" Brad whispered to Zach in perfect imitation of Philip's accent.

They sat off to one side, not to disturb her reveries, if reveries they were. She seemed not to have noticed their arrival. After a moment she mumbled something neither Brad nor Zach could catch. When she repeated the phrase, Brad thought it sounded like, "Ah'm shuah."

"Excuse me, did you say something?" he asked, reluctant to intrude on her solitude.

She swung around on them unsteadily. "Why, ah beg your pardon!" she exclaimed. "Ah didn't hear you gentlemen come in."

Brad smiled apologetically. "We have a habit of sneaking up on people. Sorry to trouble you."

"Not at all," she said. "But ah just don't know what he expects me to do. Ah mean, surely it's obvious ah'm no good for him." She waved an arm about. "Wouldn't y'all agree?"

"That depends," Zach said, "on who we're talking about."

"Why, Gerald, of course!" she said mawkishly. "We're talking about Gerald, darling. Good, kind Gerald who loves me so terribly and who ah've hurt so grievously."

Without warning, her eyes rolled up into the back of her head and she fainted dead away in the chair. Zach dashed over and felt for a pulse. She seemed to be breathing regularly. He looked at Brad and shrugged. Brad picked up her glass and sniffed.

"Mint julep," he said. "I told you. Happens every time. They're deadly."

The woman suddenly shook herself awake and regarded them with worried eyes. "Has he come back?" she asked.

"No," Brad said. "Gerald hasn't returned."

"Oh, thank goodness! Whatever will ah do when he returns?" she said, and dropped into a faint again, leaving the unanswered question hanging in the air.

Brad studied her features. She was a woman of unusual beauty and seemingly good breeding, if a little under the weather at the present moment.

Just then a slim young man appeared in the doorway. "Oh, dear me," he pronounced with an English accent. "This is not how I foresaw greeting you."

Derek came down the stairs and shook hands with them.

"A pleasure to meet you," he said to Zach, with restrained English enthusiasm. "Philip said you were a lovely boy, but I had no idea." He looked apologetically to Brad. "Dear me, I hope it's all right to say that in front of you. Don't worry— Philip and I are still madly in love." He paused and looked discomfited for a moment. "With each other, of course."

"It's perfectly fine with me," Brad said, turning to look at Zach. "I know he's adorable."

At that moment, an unmistakable hiccup came from the recumbent young woman. They all turned to look at her.

Derek shook his head. "I'm afraid Hedy has reached her limit a bit early today. She usually makes it till sundown before reaching a state of inebriation."

"She seems to be waiting for someone named Gerald," Brad offered.

"Ah, yes—the lover," Derek informed them with impeccable enunciation. "Gerald's a decent sort, but I worry she's a bit much for him. She's got him wrapped around her little finger. Hedy's a nice girl, but she's southern so there's always that other side to her. She certainly seems a bit far gone at present, poor thing."

A phone rang in the distance.

"I'll be inside," he said, heading back up the steps. "Please let me know if there's anything you need."

"What's a Brit doing running a New Orleans guesthouse?" Zach asked, watching Derek's retreating form.

"Transmigrational urges," Brad said. "He vacationed here one year and lost his heart to two different lovers."

"That can be awkward," Zach said. "Which one did he choose?"

"Both. He chose Philip *and* New Orleans. He's a much happier man than when he was living in merry-but-ever-so-slightly-damp old England, I gather. Though you'll notice no matter how much sun he gets, he never tans. Pure white skin. Like lard. It's an English thing."

Hedy snorted and thrashed in her chair. Something clattered onto the tiles at her feet. Zach stooped to pick up a key.

"Room 4," he said. "Maybe we should deposit her in bed."

"Good idea," Brad said.

Together, they manoeuvred the limp figure to a cabin just to the right of the pool. On entering, they were greeted with a very demure *miaow*. A small white cat watched them carry its mistress in with a look of curiosity and disdain. They shifted Hedy onto the bed and arranged her sleeping form on the mattress. They had just removed her shoes when she looked up and gave them a brief smile, startling in its brilliance.

"Ah thought y'all were Gerald," she said. "Y'all are beautiful, but y'all are not him, though."

No, we're not Gerald, thought Brad, remembering how he too had once passed out poolside while under the influence of bourbon. And you can be glad we're not doing this for the wrong reasons.

"*Shh!* Sleep now. Gerald will be back soon," he said soothingly.

She smiled up at him and hiccupped once more. "Y'all are so good looking. And so very kind. If y'all see Gerald, please tell him ah'm shuah. Tell him Hedy is shuah."

Brad nodded. "Tell Gerald that Hedy is sure. Will do."

"Thank you so much, kind sir!"

As they watched, the cat jumped onto the bed and kneaded the pillow at her mistress's head. Within seconds, Hedy was happily snoring away. Brad looked down and sighed. She couldn't be much more than twenty-three or twenty-four. Far too young to be drinking bourbon, he thought, feeling more than a trifle paternal.

3

Brad woke to feel Zach's erection pressed firmly against his back. Although New Orleans lacked Puerto Vallarta's rustically charming wake-up call by rooster, and the relentless shushing of waves that greeted the world-weary traveller in Provincetown, it might nevertheless be said that a certain vibrancy emanating from the very ground encouraged things more far scintillating than slumber. This was a party town, after all.

After a brief but extremely intimate "good morning", the pair dressed and slipped out to greet the sunrise while birds sang gaily in the trees. Just as they'd requested the previous night, Derek had left a pair of bicycles outside their cabin door. They hit the streets and cycled north to Lake Pontchartrain before heading east along Lakeshore Drive till it turned south through Gentilly and Bywater, then down into the Lower Ninth Ward where the storm's damage had been the most extensive. Even now, eight months after the flooding, what they saw was so formidable as to strike them almost dumb.

If true biblical retribution had ever been sent

to earth, then it might be said to have visited the Lower Ninth. It was as if the hand of God had swooped down to sideswipe the poorest of the poor. Here, Katrina's wrath was seen at its most devastating. Entire streets lay in ruin, the warped and lop-sided buildings a mute testament to the storm's destructive force. One particular house among all the others seemed to have suffered more than its neighbours. Most of the foundation had been swept away, leaving the dwelling to buckle on either side of a central support wall, where it balanced tipsily, its shutters ripped open and windows gone. The words *We Will Be Back* had been splashed in blue paint across the door, either as a warning to potential squatters or a vow to rival Scarlet O'Hara's "I'll never be hungry again!"

Strange to say, Katrina had caught many off guard. Before adopting the name she would later take down to infamy, Katrina began life as Tropical Depression Twelve, a mild disturbance that formed over the Bahamas on the evening of August 23. No one took much notice of her then or the following morning when she was upgraded from a depression to a storm and christened "Kristina." All that was soon to change, however, because the little lady was determined to leave her mark in the annals of meteorological history. Following an unexpected burst of convection, she was accorded the status of "hurricane"—the fifth of the season—just two hours before making landfall on Florida's southernmost tip.

Had the waters of the Gulf of Mexico not been so warm things might have been entirely different,

31

but after passing over mainland Florida and into the gulf, Katrina's force quickly intensified. On August 27, her radius nearly doubled, she was upgraded to a Category 3. From a purring kitten she'd turned into a roaring tiger, finally attracting the attention she wanted. And her destructive rampage had just begun.

Initial forecasts predicted a northerly path for the Kat, placing the bulk of destruction over the Florida panhandle, but she had other plans. By the following day Katrina was on a westerly trajectory heading straight for the state of Louisiana. Just past midnight on August 28 she was upgraded to a Category 4. That was when she started to gain respect as well as fear.

Katrina earned her full five stars at 7 AM the following morning, giving her a clear shot at becoming the year's most destructive storm. The Weather Forecast Office issued a strongly worded warning advising the immediate evacuation of south-eastern Louisiana and southern Mississippi. Forecasters warned of "devastating damage" and predicted the area would be "uninhabitable for weeks."

That afternoon Katrina hit her full stride, with maximum sustained winds of one hundred and seventy five miles per hour and intermittent gusts of up to two hundred and fifteen miles per hour. By the following day she would become the fourth most intense Atlantic storm on record. A clear and present danger. Only hours stood between her and New Orleans.

Meanwhile, after lengthy consultations with

the White House, marching orders came from the office of Louisiana governor Kathleen Blanco. The city's population was being firmly told—not politely asked in the usual Southern style—to get out of town. Fine for those who had transportation and could afford to go elsewhere, but many were simply too poor to comply. Others were too old. The rest were just too stubborn. They'd seen it all before. Or so they thought.

As a result, more than sixty thousand Louisianans would soon be stranded inside their sunken city with more than one million residents displaced. Fearing the worst, the city ordered "refuges of last resort" to be made available for those who would or could not leave, including the more than twenty-six thousand folks who eventually took shelter inside the Louisiana Superdome.

Far out at sea, a lonely buoy recorded a breathtaking fifty-five-foot wave surge, one of the highest ever. But it wasn't at sea that attention was now focused. At 6:10 AM on August 29, Katrina made her second call on land and proceeded to eat her way up the Louisiana coast. The Kat was now officially the third most powerful hurricane to hit the United States, with a sure bet at becoming the most costly.

New Orleans didn't stand a chance.

One by one, the levees and floodwalls protecting the city failed in a total of fifty-three places, leaving eighty percent of the city under water. Before the crisis was over, more than a thousand people would die, with almost another thousand officially missing. Sixty-two tornadoes would be recorded across eight states as a result of her passing. Two days later, apparently satisfied, Katrina was quietly subsumed by a low-pressure system below the Great Lakes. But her tale wasn't over.

More than sixty thousand people were now trapped inside the sunken city without adequate food and water, nearly half of them in the Superdome. That was when the story began to get personal. From the outset, recovery operations were hampered by extreme conditions and the dangers posed by boating through a drowned metropolis. The water was rank with the decay of bloated corpses. Added to this was the ever-present menace of alligators and poisonous snakes while from above, oblivious to all suffering, the sun beat down relentlessly, turning the city into a stewing cauldron of death and decay.

Twice the levees were repaired and twice they were breached again. By the time recovery operations were in full swing, the advanced state of decomposition of many of the corpses—some of which had been in the water for days—hindered even the most obdurate efforts to identify them.

Now, eight months later, the empty streets were a mute testimony to the devastation. Houses made rank with mould, their floors and walls swollen by moisture, had simply collapsed. Entire sections of sidewalks had crumpled, while the sea walk was missing in places. Elsewhere, streetlights bent to the sidewalk like religious postulants prostrating themselves. A church steeple hung at right angles to the ground, shaken from its former place of divine authority. Some days it looked as though the city might never recover.

A sense of hopelessness hung in the air. Defeat showed on everyone's face. There seemed no end to the misery or reminders of what had happened. When recovery operations commenced, every building in the city limits was spray painted with a large circle divided in four quadrants. The initials of the first rescue agency to arrive were noted on the left, with the date above. The right-hand quadrant listed potential hazards on the site, while the bottom indicated the number of survivors found or, if none, the number of corpses. Many found the markings eerily reminiscent of tattoos on concentration-camp victims.

In the initial weeks of the rescue, street numbers were stripped from house fronts. Now they were being replaced by returning inhabitants hoping for mail service and other unthinkable luxuries. Unfortunately, a number displayed on a house marked it with an open invitation to steal and plunder. Looting became the city's latest plague, as building supplies brought in by day vanished overnight. The crime rate soared.

Their dispiriting tour of duty over, Brad and Zach cycled back to the Lion's Roar. Wheeling alongside the inn, they were accompanied by the ubiquitous pack of dogs falling over one another in an effort to inform the newcomers of backyard etiquette. As they made their way to the cabin, Brad and Zach passed the sadly beautiful Hedy, once again reclining beside the pool. A man with a bushy moustache and wary eyes sat watching over her like a small but earnest bear on guard duty.

Despite the sun, dark circles showed beneath Hedy's eyes. Her skin was pale almost to the point of translucence. Brad decided to revise his description of her from the previous day, but only slightly. While her profile and jawline remained stubbornly Kate Hepburn, her eyes were pure Tallulah Bankhead—big and moony, with a perpetually dissatisfied stare.

"Good mawning, gentlemen," she greeted.

"Good morning, Hedy," Brad said.

She looked him up and down, throwing an anxious glance at her companion. "Have we met before, sir?"

"Yesterday in fact, but only in passing," Brad said, to dispel her discomfort. "I'm Brad and this is my partner Zach."

Hedy flashed a brilliant smile. "Charmed," she said, reaching a slender hand across the table. "Please forgive mah dreadful lapse of memory and terrible manners. This is mah *friend* Gerald."

The italics spoke volumes.

Gerald stood and offered a hand to the pair. "Nice to meet you," he said quietly.

Just then the perpetually affable Derek emerged from the house bearing a tray of glasses and steaming biscuits. "Fresh-squeezed orange juice and Philip's hushpuppies to start the morning," he announced, setting the tray on the table. "Help yourselves, please. May I get anything for anyone?"

Hedy looked up and beamed a helpless smile. "Y'all are such a darling man, but ah am in need of absolutely nothing at the present moment..."

Derek turned to go inside.

"But..."

Derek turned back.

She smiled sadly and held up a glass. "Maybe just an eentsie-weentsie dash of bourbon to freshen up mah orange juice?"

"Now, Hedy." Gerald gave her a warning look. "It's too early to start drinking."

"*Please*, darling!" she murmured, batting her eyelashes in a way that Brad thought had gone out of fashion with corsets. "Why, it's nearly eleven in the AM!"

Gerald hesitated, but his lovesickness was clearly stronger than his resolve. "Of course, my darling. Anything for you."

Derek produced a flask from his jacket pocket and gave a little wink. "I had a suspicion someone might be in need," he said, pouring a generous splash into her glass.

Without bothering to stir the drink, she sipped and murmured approvingly. Derek nodded and retreated to the inn.

Hedy turned her smile on Brad. "Now don't make fun of me because ah forget things easily. What brings y'all to N'Orleans?"

"Just a little vacation. We wanted to see how the restoration efforts are going."

Hedy's smile faded. "Not so terribly well, as y'all must have seen by now."

"We took a bike tour through the city this

morning," Zach said. "The devastation is breathtaking. It must be disheartening for the people who live here."

Hedy shook her head. "Some days ah think they'll never get this city back on its feet." She fluttered a hand in Gerald's direction. "But y'all should talk to Gerald about it. Gerald was with FEMA. He knows how badly everything is being mismanaged."

Gerald nodded and helped himself to one of Philip's airy-looking biscuits.

"It's a real scandal," he said, his accent entirely free of any southern inflection. "It's like they're throwing money at the walls and hoping things will fix themselves."

Hedy waved an arm encouragingly. "Go on, Gerald. Tell them about the public housing. The entire world must hear of this abomination."

Gerald took a breath. "We've just learned that the Department of Housing and Urban Development is sending in bulldozers to tear down low-cost public housing that would be cheaper to fix than to replace—"

"Bulldozers!" Hedy cried, her eyes flashing. "Can y'all imagine? They are going to raze hundreds of buildings to the ground, but there are no plans to replace them. It's a disgrace. There'll be nowhere for low-income families to live in this city. None at all. They simply won't be able to afford to return."

Gerald nodded. "It's pure corruption. A friend of one of the biggest project managers got the contract without even tendering a public bid. Hedy wised me up to what was going on. I was with FEMA at the time, but Hedy convinced me to leave."

"It's disgusting," she proclaimed. "Ah said he ought to have been ashamed to work for them, but when ah told Gerald what they were doing, why, he quit right on the spot!"

Gerald reached a sympathetic hand across the table and took Hedy's fingers in his big bear paw. Brad's ears were burning. Grace had told them to look into reconstruction irregularities, and this fit the bill.

"If ah had my way," Hedy continued, "they'd be housing people in those abandoned warehouses down along the river. Right now, they are standing completely empty! Can you imagine? With all those poor people living under causeways and highway ramps, ah just don't understand it. It's a terrible, terrible disgrace! Whatever is wrong with this government?"

"But surely FEMA must be getting something done," Brad suggested.

Hedy shook her head impatiently. "It doesn't matter," she insisted. "They're not doing the *right* things. And ah know why! If that Willard Foster doesn't stop—"

Gerald threw her a cautionary look. Hedy put a hand to her mouth and looked over at him.

"Ah know, darling. Ah know ah'm not supposed to speak of it."

Hedy downed her drink. At a nod from Gerald, the two of them stood.

"It's been an honour, gentlemen," Hedy said.

"When dare ah look forward to the pleasure of our next meeting?"

"Very soon, I'm sure," Brad said, feeling his manners seriously flawed in the face of Hedy's extravagant phrasing. "We're here for a week, possibly more. I'm sure we'll run into each other again."

"Ah'm utterly charmed," she said.

"Gentlemen," Gerald said with a nod.

And with that, the pair wandered off down the path.

Derek emerged in time to see them go. "I see you're getting acquainted with Hedy," he said.

"In a manner of speaking," Brad replied. "She seems not to remember us from yesterday."

"It's probably just as well," Zach said with a grin. "We helped her undress and put her to bed."

Derek looked off after the vanished couple. "I'm not surprised. She's drowning herself in alcohol trying to escape a failed marriage. Gerald's a nice boy, terribly polite, but he's young and a bit too impressionable. And not really her type, I suspect. Still, I gather he intends to rescue Hedy from herself. I just hope he doesn't drown himself in the attempt."

Brad nodded. "In her drunken state yesterday, she told us to tell him that she was sure."

Derek looked up in curiosity. "Sure of what?"

"I don't know, but she sounded pretty serious when she said it."

They all looked with concern in the direction of the hapless Hedy, as though her fragile femininity might require their combined attention.

40

Derek shook his head in a motherly fashion. "She's a sad case. When we met just a few years ago, she was leader of the Young Republicans in Louisiana. She was an idealist, full of fire and enthusiasm, and working for a man she thought would do a lot of good." He sighed. "I gather lately she's lost her taste for politics. She resigned last month and has since become known as something of a maverick around town. She's got a few people worried by her outspokenness. It's largely fuelled by alcohol, as you might have guessed."

He began gathering up the empty glasses.

"Who is Willard Foster?" Brad asked.

Derek paused in his actions. "Not a nice man, by all accounts, but an extremely wealthy one. He was Hedy's boss till she resigned. Since then she's been doing her best to damage his reputation. I gather she feels he's done things that are close to being illegal since the reconstruction process."

"Such as?" Zach asked.

"Questionable project tendering is one of the rumours you hear. But it's not the only one." Derek shrugged. "It wouldn't be Louisiana without graft and bribery. The politicians are famous for it. There are a lot of questionable things going on here."

"We had a good tour of the city this morning. I'd hoped it would be in better shape by now," Brad said.

Zach nodded. "Clearly, the rumours are true. You've been abandoned by your government."

Derek sighed and sat down. "Some days it seems so. The Federal Emergency Management

Agency is trying to make things happen. I understand Gerald was working for them till Hedy convinced him to stop. She believes FEMA is doing all the wrong things. She may be right. The organization has a bad reputation here among the locals. The joke is that FEMA stands for 'Fix Everything My Ass.' That's not far off the truth, as fixing seems to be the last thing they're doing."

Brad cast a glance around the grounds. "At least the inn seems to have held up well."

Derek nodded sheepishly. "Philip and I were lucky. We got out in time, but others didn't. There was no electricity or running water for weeks. You couldn't even flush a toilet. Rapes and lootings were common. Snipers shot at people boating over the water trying to get to shelter. It was a war zone. We came back when the worst was over. There was only a little flooding in the Marigny because we're above sea level here, but the city is still a disaster and that affects all of us. When you look around you don't see too many happy, smiley people anymore."

Brad nodded. "I'm sure it's difficult to believe, but the city will get back on its feet one day."

"I hope so," Derek said. "Here and there you see its spirit coming back to life. It's like a flame you thought had died, but refuses to give up." A look of worry crossed his stoical features. "But the city isn't the same. We're all uneasy about the future. We wait and wait, but little seems to be happening to help us. Hope is running out for a lot of people. Too many broken promises..."

"It takes time to fulfil promises," Brad

reminded him.

"Naturally. FEMA offered trailers to anyone who wanted to return, but they promised more than they could deliver." He looked off into the distance in a way that reminded Brad of Hedy's vacant stare. "A lot of the folks who came back are homeless. Even though some of them have jobs, they can't afford to live anywhere. Some formed tent cities and others are camping out under bridges, but things are getting more desperate as time goes on. It's like a frontier mentality. People feel abandoned, and with good reason." He shrugged. "As I said, Philip and I got off easy. We pretty much returned to our old lives once the flooding abated, but others lost everything. They've changed. It's like they don't know you any more. I saw an old friend and waved at him the other day. He just walked on by like he had no idea who I was. It was odd."

"Shell shock," Brad said. "There's a lot to absorb and sift through after what's happened. It must take quite a bit of getting used to."

Derek shook his head. "There's that, of course. And then there are the disappeared—nobody knows where they went or even if they got away. There are more than a thousand names on the missing-persons lists."

At that moment, a cabin door opened. A young man in cut-off shorts and a T-shirt that hugged his muscular torso emerged carrying a bucket and a mop. With his razzle-dazzle cheekbones and robin's egg-blue eyes, he was youthful perfection personified. He looked up at the sun, yawning and stretching. His smile flashed like heat lightning

"That big yellow ball surely is a wonder, ain't it?" he asked. He had an accent like an egg sizzling on the hood of a black sedan in ninety-degree heat.

"Have you finished the cabins yet?" Derek asked.

The boy nodded. "It's all coochie hoochie, Derek."

Derek smiled. "You mean hoochie coochie. Yes, it sure is that." He turned to Brad and Zach. "These are our new guests, Bradford and Zachary," Derek said. "And this is our new houseboy, Quint."

"It's a pleasure to meet y'all," Quint said, extending a hand.

Before Brad could grasp it, a frown crossed the boy's face. He withdrew the appendage and examined his palm. It was streaked with dirt. "Take care!" he cried, his expression fearful.

He wiped the hand earnestly on his cut-offs and examined it again. When he saw that most of the dirt had been rubbed off, he grinned like a Caravaggio cherub and proceeded to shake hands with the guests.

"Don't want to get you all messy, like. Me an' the dirt get down to it at times, if you know what I mean."

Brad smiled. "I know what you mean," he said, feeling drawn to the boy's dazzling eyes.

Bradford melted as Quint flashed another devastating smile. He wanted to pick him up and mother him.

Just then Quint grasped his pail handle and turned to Derek. "Ah'll get the laundry in next and after that's done ah'll skim the pool," he said.

"That's wonderful, Quint. You are a great worker."

The boy beamed. "Thanks kindly, Derek. Ah sure am grateful to you."

Brad watched the houseboy turn a corner then he let out a breath. "Whew! For a minute there, I could hardly breathe."

"He's certainly a beauty, isn't he?" Derek asked. "He's also the best worker we've ever had."

"Where'd you find him?" Brad asked.

"Quint's another sad case," Derek said. "He showed up out of nowhere a few months ago. One night, Philip and I heard a commotion at the front door. We went out and found him lying on the porch. He'd been beaten badly and left for dead in what we think was a queer bashing. We took him to the hospital, but he had no money or identification so Philip and I paid the medical bill ourselves. Afterwards, we brought him back here to recover. He seems to have adopted us." He smiled. "And we him, of course. He's a bit simple, as you've no doubt gathered. I think he suffered amnesia in the attack, possibly even brain damage. All he knew was that his name was Quint. He doesn't seem to remember where he came from or what he did before he arrived at our door."

"So many lost people," Brad said. "Where is the silver lining to Katrina's tragedy, I wonder?"

"It's hard to find one," Derek agreed. "At least the city's still here."

"I wish we could do something to help," Brad said.

Derek brightened. "Actually, there is something you can do. We're having a Derelict Disco Spirit Raising Party tomorrow night. It's going to be held in one of the old warehouses down by the river. We've found some local musicians to play and a few politicians and city workers are coming out to talk about raising funds for the disaster relief. It should be a blast."

"Count us in!" Zach exclaimed. "We're always ready to help a good cause."

"Who could turn down a party in N'Orleans?" Brad seconded.

"Maybe I'll finally get to try some bourbon," Zach said, looking at his boyfriend. "If Brad loosens up a bit, that is."

Brad scowled. "We'll see. That could be a bit too much spirit raising."

4

The inn's only other guests were a gay Japanese couple given to enthusiastic declarations that sounded like, "We love Dixieland!" but which might actually have been, "We love Disneyland!" On emerging from their cabin, the pair introduced themselves as Mr. Nobutsugo and Mr. Sakamoto. They were exceedingly polite, smooth-skinned and pretty. They claimed, as Philip had said, to be in New Orleans to find "some bees." After a few exploratory bites of the hushpuppies and a cautious sip of orange juice, they too were off.

Otherwise, with the exception of Hedy and her *friend* Gerald, the Lion's Roar was empty. It was, Brad noted, a stark change from pre-Katrina days, when the inn was booked months in advance and guests came and went at all hours with waves and friendly greetings. Now it felt more like an exclusive members' club than an ordinary B&B. Harsh new times, harsh new realities.

With little else to do that afternoon, Agents Red and Kong lounged by the pool. Brad slipped into safety mode, avoiding the sun and imbibing no more than one mint julep, though he allowed Zach a double mojito. The drink had minimal effect on his partner, however. Already laid back, Zach appeared only slightly more relaxed than usual in contrast to Brad's high-strung nature.

At four o'clock, Brad took a few minutes to update their boss on what they'd learned about the reconstruction process. She listened quietly as he gave his report.

"By the way, they've got a really funny nickname for FEMA down here," Bradford told her.

"Fix Everything My Ass?" Grace asked, before he could deliver the punch line.

"Uh, yeah. I guess you heard."

"Blame the comedy circuit," she said. "Still, it sounds like an interesting tip. I suggest you ask about this Willard Foster fellow. It never hurts to follow the money and see where it leads."

"Anything else?"

"Yes. I suggest you watch your bourbon intake while you're down there. I noticed an interesting red flag on your file in that regard."

"Oh, no, that was years ago! Just a casual weekend at Southern Decadence," Brad said, shocked to learn such things were in his file. "Don't worry. I've given it up."

"Harrumph," Grace said, leaving Brad to wonder just how omniscient his boss really was.

Later that evening, Brad and Zach went in search of a working restaurant in the French Quarter. Despite numerous closures, tantalizing odours enticed from all sides. One thing was sure: New Orleans hadn't lost its flare for cuisine.

The Creole Gumbo House won them over. Dressed in a shimmery kaftan, with glittery eyeshadow and a bunch of grapes draped over one ear, the hostess reminded Brad of a cross between Yvonne De Carlo and Carmen Miranda. She seemed to be one of those straight women who thought that competing with drag queens was a winnable proposition.

The restaurant boasted a full house. Elegant diners relaxed in candlelit tableaux as waiters in white tuxes scurried about fulfilling their wishes. Bradford rested his chin on his hand and gazed contentedly across the table at his boyfriend. Wearing a burgundy shirt, smart black trousers, and with his hair slicked back, he might have stepped straight from a Christian Dior ad. Meanwhile, a white sailor's top neatly framed Zach's trim torso over a pair of urban-adventure cargo shorts, adding a touch of street cred to the Burberry Prorsum look. Brad knew himself to be a lucky guy. He'd always been sceptical of the phrase "I'd give my life for you", but since meeting Zach he knew it to be true of him in the most literal sense. He would willingly have done so, and was certain Zach felt the same.

Their waiter made a demure appearance, outlining the evening's specials with evocative hand gestures and twinkling eyes. Zach opted for the Cajun shrimp *étouffée*, while Brad's choice of grilled alligator *au citron* made Zach's eyebrows rise.

"Don't tell me you're getting squeamish," Brad said.

"Nah." Zach shook his head. "I'm just surprised you would eat something that could easily eat you."

"I draw the line at blackened grizzly gizzards. But I hope you're not suggesting I've become boring since we met."

Zach grinned. "Not at all. It's been the most exciting time of my life."

"No regrets then?" Brad asked, wondering if his influence on his partner would always be a good thing. He'd made it abundantly clear it was against his wishes when Zach joined Box 77, though he was secretly glad he had. Who could say what the future held, for good or evil?

Zach smiled. "None whatsoever. I told you already, I'm in it for the long haul—with you and the organization."

Brad reached across the table and squeezed Zach's hand. "Good."

Just then the waiter returned with their bottle of wine. He winked, popped and poured.

Brad took a sip. "Exquisite!"

"Splendid!" The waiter topped them up and left.

Brad raised his cup. "To our first official operation together," he said.

"To our first official and *successful* operation," Zach added, as they clinked glasses.

Sitting in shadows a few tables away, a man turned at the sound of the words. His skin was pocked and a silver earring dangled from his left ear. One side of his head was shaved right down to the skull. Bold new fashion or pre-operative state, it was hard to say. Several times over the course of the evening, Brad thought the man was staring at them. Whenever he looked over, however, he merely appeared to be gazing off into the distance.

The meal ended with a double serving of flourless chocolate-bourbon cake. This gentle introduction to the disreputable liquor, Brad explained, would not prove such a bad influence on Zach. Tellingly, it was one of the few times Brad allowed himself to indulge his craving for desserts without bemoaning the state of his waistline, impeccably lean to all eyes but his own.

"Chocolate and bourbon," he said. "Who knew they could combine two of the deadliest ingredients known to man?"

After dinner, feeling relaxed and cheery, they toured the downtown circuit, a six-block radius containing almost as much novelty as all of Manhattan. Stilt walkers towered above the crowds, living statues in silver body paint posed for photographs, and sidewalk artists painted masterpieces to order. Elsewhere, horse-drawn buggies offered rides to the nostalgic and gypsies foretold futures for the love-struck. On every other corner, clowns clowned, dancers danced and jugglers juggled. New Orleans was living up to its reputation as "the greatest free show on earth."

In the midst of it all, Bourbon Street belched its concoction of musical gumbo. Fleet-fingered zydeco musicians wailed and Dixieland bands marched past the open-air bars and clubs. As though daring Katrina to return, *The Levee Breaking Blues* was just one of many melodic strains being tossed about that evening. Brad loved the gaucherie and brashness of it all, even as he found his musical sensibility rubbed raw with the kaleidoscope of clashing tunes and discordant keys. It was *Charge of the Light Brigade* crossed with a fleet of racing fire engines and wheezing oompah bands that would give Charles Ives a run for his money. Every once in a while, he stopped and put his fingers to his ears. There was no use trying to make sense of it. It simply had to be accepted.

New Orleans was the only city Brad knew where the streets talked, if you knew how to listen. And, oh, the stories they told! Tales of the slave trade and the new world's first elected black official, of the birthplace of Dixieland and more genuine jazz musicians than almost any other town. Long before that most infamous N'Orleans trio—Tennessee Williams, Blanche Dubois and Stanley Kowalski—breezed into town and turned the place upside down, it was already a gay Mecca. Lately it had become even more so with the rise of Southern Decadence, when thousands of naked and half-naked gay men roamed the streets, strutting and preening like peacocks to the outraged gasps of the uninitiated. The folks from Wichita and Scranton who stumbled unawares into the midst of this sensual free-for-all would never be the same again. No great loss, some would say. Not to mention the gain of the occasional liberated spirit who chose to return for a second round of decadence in the future. For all intents and purposes, it was a modern gay Shangri-La shimmying out its moment in the sun.

"I just love it here," Brad exclaimed, grabbing Zach in a frisky embrace. "And I just love being here with you!"

The city had a way of bringing out an uncharacteristic ardour in visitors, creating a tingling that made them feel youthful and alive, no matter their age or state of virility. It emboldened and enflamed even the quietest of natures with a desire to do strange things and—sometimes—to talk about them afterwards.

"I think it's time to introduce you to the genuine article," Brad declared, grabbing Zach by the hand and pointing to a sign reading *Bourbon Orleans*.

The bar exhaled a dusky wreath of tobacco fumes as they entered. Unlike the rest of the civilized world, in New Orleans smoking was considered a right. Clinging to its French heritage, the city proclaimed *la cigarette* a necessity to health and well-being. Here, smoking was a sacred institution. Just as sex without passion was unthinkable to a native N'Orleaner, so too drink without smoke was inconceivable. Let New York, Los Angeles, Chicago, and even funny little Toronto have their neurotic health concerns. Here, there were no smoking bans. Nor could there ever be. *Fumer, c'est moi!* declared the residents. Trying to change it would have brought on a second Battle of New Orleans.

Behind the counter, bare-chested bartenders scurried to a pounding beat. To a man, they were dressed in shorts so tight you could call them at a glance: left-hanging, right-dangling or up-slung. The effect was to make the clientele quaff their drinks as quickly as possible in order to return to watch their favourites dash back and forth with lubricious efficiency, even if they couldn't spell it. At least, the tourists did. Native N'Orleaners never hurried, imbibing in a mellow haze of good times and good cheer, with an inertia that could rival a desert tortoise's. Today was today and tomorrow was an unthinkable glimmer on the horizon. Before they got to that horizon, however, there was a whole lot of bourbon to be had for the asking. So really, friend, what was your hurry?

Attention wavered as a spotlight cut a brilliant hole at the far end of the bar. A gaudy RuPaul look-a-like emerged from behind the curtain, stopping to pose like a 40s *Vogue* model as she surveyed the crowd.

"Are y'all havin' a good time?" she asked, to scattered cheering. With size-large hands firmly clamped to her hips, she turned an exacting eye on the crowd. "Gentlemen, y'all are in *N'Orleans*! Is that the best y'all can do?"

At this, the cheering turned to a roar.

"That's better, though I'm willing to bet by the time tonight is over y'all are gonna be shoutin' a good deal louder than that. *Laissez les bon ton roulet,* gentlemen. Let the good times roll! Y'all are gonna be a long time dead, so don't wait to enjoy your pleasures. Speaking of which, I would like to introduce you to one of the greatest pleasures I know. Please make some noise and give a big N'Orleans welcome to a true gentleman and a legend among strippers!"

Howls filled the room and the queen sashayed backwards off-stage to a slithery beat. Shimmering cymbals gave way to a sinuous melody as a muscular arm reached through the curtain, swaying like a snake. The arm was joined by its mate and the curtains parted to reveal a figure in a hooded gown like a character out of *Scheherazade*. Even in this tent-like getup, the crowd knew they were looking at a bodybuilder with a stunning physique. He was a hottie in a *djellaba*.

Swaying to the beat, the dancer teased the garment up an inch at a time, revealing a circlet of bells around each ankle, then further till it reached his knees. A collective sigh went up at the sight of massive calves, like the twin pillars of Hercules, flexing and jangling with every move.

The *djellaba* floated upward past spectacular thighs to reveal the holy of holies, a silver pouch lovingly clasping the dancer's crotch. With each movement, the jiggling package was thrust up and out like a promise offered then retracted again. Judging by the bulge, the promise was formidable.

An awed hush overtook the room—no mean feat with a bar crowd. A veteran of strip-show audiences, Brad was not easily impressed by such feats, however, and with Zach at his side neither was he inclined to be enticed by other men. But this particular stripper had succeeded in capturing his full attention.

With one swift movement the garment was rent along its Velcro seams and tossed aside, followed by an immediate and deafening roar from the crowd. The dancer's body was nothing less than stupendous. Each muscle was toned to perfection, every movement calculated to show off the man's breathtaking features except for two: his privates tucked enticingly inside the silver pouch, and his face, which remained hidden by a silk *niqab*.

Brad suspected the dancer was a closeted professional who practiced burlesque by night while working as a mild-mannered doctor, accountant or dentist by day. Or perhaps, Brad thought, he was one of those unfortunates with a spectacular body and unspeakable face, afraid to show himself for fear of ruining the fantasy: the perfect physique married to a face that could shut down a nuclear power plant.

The music changed. The dancer spun on his heels, offering the crowd a view of a flawless backside tattooed with twin scorpions. So perfectly sculpted were the two globes that they might have made a grown cowboy cry. The crowd hooted and cheered.

Even Zach had grown uncharacteristically restive. "Wow! That's one hot daddy," he exclaimed, belying his usual cool reserve.

Bradford, meanwhile, had gone totally silent, projected back to a wintry landscape in rural Indiana one cold and memorable night many long years before. It started like this: sometime in the course of his foreshortened adolescence, Brad had managed to filch a skin magazine of the gay variety, a rarity for boys under the age of fourteen. Nightly, he devoured its pages one gleaming photograph at a time. In the middle, folded discreetly, was a model so sizzling he took Brad's breath away. His eyes were mesmeric, his cheekbones sardonic, his pecs prodigious, and his endowment magnificent. The same man served as young Bradford's undercover companion for many a long night that year and well into the next.

From that day onward, young Brad kept his eyes peeled for subsequent incarnations of the same model. And he found them. The man appeared in a variety of settings and states of undress, in spreads of black and white and full colour, shaved and hirsute. He lay sprawled on fire escapes and draped across the backs of pick-up trucks, popping the corks of champagne bottles and lifting bales of hay. Once he appeared in a chef's costume amid a gleaming galley kitchen, disrobing utensil by utensil while serving up a delectable feast. Sadly, Brad lamented, gone were the days of whimsically salacious porn shoots created by visionary set decorators with impossibly high standards. These days it was all gymnasium change rooms and mechanic's garages, surroundings that were serviceable but entirely uninspired, and therefore risible, as far as Brad was concerned. *Sic transit* etc.

Over the course of the model's career, every inch of his spectacularity had been rendered up to the prying eyes of the voyeur. Rather than satiate desire, however, each image created an appetite for more, as though it were not possible to present this man in enough carnal variations to satisfy the collective need.

On coming across his first porn tapes in his later teens, Brad discovered the same model in a solo set-up pleasuring himself in a steamy sauna. Poses that once moved only in Brad's mind now sprang to life in real-time. Yet, somehow, Brad sensed there was more to this man's perfection than self-pleasure. In the magazines and videos he remained untouchable, staring out from the page or the screen as though yearning to escape. It struck Brad what that yearning was: loneliness, pure and simple. In all those years of offering himself up to the camera lens, he had never once appeared with anyone else.

To Brad the man was an archetype. And archetypes were by their very nature solitary, exemplary symbols of perfection. One of a kind. In a class by himself. That was what this man was. Such men were unattainable to mere mortals like Bradford Fairfax.

Then, quite suddenly and unexpectedly, the fantasy came to life one night when Brad walked into a small bar in Indiana. He'd just turned twenty-one and was unworldly in sexual matters. Till then he had been satisfied by awkward gropings in the dark with other inexperienced young men like himself, but all that was about to change forever. He found himself in a small club on a darkened side street with a marquee advertising *Harlan Masterson—Gentleman Stripper*. Brad watched, incredulous, as the lights went up and he found himself in the presence of his fantasy man, come to life. All through the act he felt as though Harlan were stripping for one person, and one person only: Bradford Fairfax.

The act ended and the fanfare began. Brad turned to order another beer, stunned by what he'd just seen. A moment later, Harlan reappeared in the club, fully dressed. He walked up to Brad and grabbed his hand.

"You don't belong here," he said. "And neither do I. Let's clear out."

It was all the invitation Brad needed.

That night, Harlan proved to the young Bradford that not only did lonely porn stars occasionally need to be with real flesh-and-blood men, but also that sometimes the man they wanted to be with was Bradford Fairfax. A whirlwind date in a roadside motel, a cheap bottle of wine, and a highly memorable and utilitarian lassoing session ensued. Brad was in ecstasy all night long. He'd met his fantasy man in the flesh.

The next day Harlan moved on, as fantasy lovers do, leaving behind an empty wine bottle, a sweaty T-shirt, a few rope burns and the indelible memory of that fulfilling night—a memory that had so far lasted more than a decade. With any luck, it might last a lifetime. Brad had come away with one other recollection from that long, delirious evening: twin scorpions tattooed on Harlan's immaculate buttocks.

The body gyrated before them, naked except for a silver thong and a *niqab*, that tiny veil of modesty preventing the face from being seen by the heathen, a curtain separating man from God. The flesh made inviolable.

With one deft twist of the wrist, the *niqab* was

torn aside and Brad's fantasy became flesh again. Instantly, he recognized the man he'd yearned for all those years ago before finally meeting him for one brief but unforgettable night of splendour when he'd glimpsed something more sweetly compelling even than the face of Ishtar.

Sensing his partner's unusually silent turn, Zach turned to him with concern. "Are you all right? You look as though you'd seen a ghost."

"A ghost of my past," Brad said, nodding to the figure vanishing off-stage right. "That was Harlan Masterson—Gentleman Stripper."

Without a second thought, he rushed backstage. The dressing room was empty, the door standing open onto the hallway. Harlan always made a fast escape.

"Drat! I missed him," Brad said dolefully.

Outside the club, he looked up at the marquee: *Harlan Masterson—Gentleman Stripper. One Night Only!* Somehow he'd overlooked it on the way in.

It was past midnight by the time Brad and Zach returned to the Faubourg Marigny. Out of the downtown core the streets retreated into silence, except once they passed a vacant lot where an unseen fountain splashed playfully in the darkness, hosting an orchestra of bullfrogs piping out a Philip Glass symphony.

They walked on to the Lion's Roar and slipped inside the gate. If they'd turned their heads, they might have seen a figure standing under the branches of a sweetbay magnolia on the opposite side of the street. And if the figure had turned its head, they would have seen that one side was shaved right down to the scalp.

5

His astonishment at seeing Harlan again kept Brad talking till late. Having lost both parents by the age of fifteen, and with no other living relatives, Brad had few significant personal signposts in his past. Harlan Masterson was one of them. Fortunately for Brad, Zach wasn't a jealous lover. He clearly understood the place of *other* significant others in Brad's past, as few as they were. Brad went on at length to explain the positive effects Harlan had had on him, how that one evening had been an act of true liberation, raising the curtain on both his sexual and emotional life. It forever separated him from the lonely boy he'd been, the one who stood waiting in the wings silently wishing for something good to happen to him. Because it *had* happened and that something was Harlan.

Brad looked over to discover Zach had fallen asleep during his monologue. He smiled, his heart warmed by the sight, even if whatever he'd said had been lost on his blue-haired amour. He turned out the light and slipped in under the covers beside him.

That night he was plagued by an eerie dream. In it, he found himself cycling along the banks of the Mississippi River in the Lower Ninth Ward where the devastation had been greatest. Each street he turned down was empty, the slithering of his wheels beneath him the only sound. As he rode along, the water rose to his toes, then his ankles and calves. Brad pedalled frantically, desperate to gain higher ground. Puffing and straining, he reached the boundary of the next ward. There he was startled to see a sign reading, "You Are Leaving the City of the Dead. Thanks for Stopping By."

He woke shivering. Real or imagined, the City of the Dead was a terrifying place.

Zach snored gently as Brad crept out of bed and headed to the shower. His lover was still asleep when Brad emerged drying himself with a towel. Better to let him rest, he thought, as he stepped out into the early morning light, soft and gentle where it caressed the branches overhead.

He made his way to the pool, expecting to find it deserted. As he approached, however, a disturbing sound reached his ears. Someone was crying in the garden. He peered around a corner to see Quint sitting on the tiles beside the goldfish pond. The boy was sobbing his eyes out.

Hedy knelt beside him. "It's all right, baby," she said, smoothing his cheeks. "Nothing can hurt him now."

The body of a rabbit lay across Quint's knees. He stroked its ears absently, tears flowing down his face.

63

"It's ended," he said mournfully, as though the death of this rabbit signified not just the death of one small rodent but the demise of an entire species.

Hedy looked up at Brad.

"A traffic casualty, ah believe," she said, in reply to his unspoken question. "One of the dogs dragged it in from the street."

"Take care," Quint whimpered.

"Yes, take care," Brad said. "It's all right. Nothing can hurt him now."

"Quint gets very upset when anything dies," Hedy explained. "He's such a dear, gentle soul."

"We have to bury him," Quint said, looking balefully up at the sky. "Before the big yellow ball goes away."

Hedy nodded. "Ah'll get the Popsicle stick."

She rose and headed to the inn.

Quint continued to stroke the rabbit's fur. "Dog says we need to bury things when they end. Dog sees everything. When something ends, we need to bury it so the devils can't eat its soul."

Brad nodded, though he found the boy's outlook on life somewhat alarming. Probably raised a Southern Baptist, he told himself. Hedy returned with a Popsicle stick and a magic marker.

"What should we name it, Quint?"

Quint cocked his head and looked thoughtful. "Sextus," he replied after a moment.

Hedy knelt and wrote the letters S-E-X-T-U-S lengthwise on the stick.

Quint stood, cradling the rabbit in his arms. He skirted the pond, heading to the back of the garden where the greenery was densest. Hedy and Brad followed him through a cleft in the bushes. In the middle of a small clearing, Brad found himself looking down on rows of Popsicle sticks jutting up from the earth. It appeared to be a miniature graveyard.

"He likes to bury things," Hedy explained. "Mice, butterflies, gecko lizards ... even some of the goldfish from the pond. When something dies it just worries him no end."

Quint knelt and began scooping out a hole with his fingers, then he laid the rabbit on its side and smoothed its fur one last time. When it was covered with earth, he jammed the Popsicle stick upright in the dirt.

"Our Mother who art a heathen, hollow be thy mane. Please take Sextus to your loving place and look after him," Quint intoned softly.

Brad's brow furrowed. What on earth went on in this boy's brain?

Quint looked up with his startling blue eyes. "Better now," he said. "Sextus is safe. The devils won't get him."

His eyes suddenly went vacant, as though someone had turned off a light. He stood and moved dumbly away.

"It breaks mah heart," Hedy said, looking after him. "Ah just wish ah could do more for him."

Brad studied her for a moment, recalling their brief conversation the previous day. He wondered what else Hedy could tell him about what was really going on in New Orleans.

As though she'd read his thoughts, she said,

"Y'all were asking about the reconstruction process. The South will rise again, as they say, but ah believe y'all were referring specifically to N'Orleans."

"I was."

She looked him directly in the eye. "It's time for me to speak mah mind about the terrible unfairness goin' on. Truth is, it's the contractors and lawyers and politicians who are benefiting here, not the people who lost everything. Without affordable housing, this will become a city of the elite."

"It's certainly happened elsewhere," Brad agreed.

"Yes, but what you may not realize is that there is much more at stake here than just the destruction of affordable public housing. Much more even than the end of hope for the future of working-class N'Orleaners to return to their homes. Ah may be young, but ah'm not naïve about any of this."

Brad nodded. "Louisiana's a pretty rough-and-tumble state. I gather the politics can get a bit nasty down here."

"That is precisely the problem." Hedy tossed her head defiantly. "And our politicians are hell bent on giving their friends and business associates every opportunity to make hay while the sun shines."

Brad listened, but said nothing. This wasn't news, he reminded himself. Certainly not here, at any rate. Before Hedy could say more, however, Gerald's voice cut through the air. Her bravado vanished suddenly, her expression turning to habitual sadness once again.

"We're over here, darlin'," she called with an apologetic glance at Brad.

Brad followed her back through the garden, swatting aside giant ferns and hibiscus branches. The burly construction worker stood by the pool, looking suspiciously from Brad to Hedy and back again.

"Good morning," he said to Brad, taking Hedy by the arm and marching her a little ways off.

Without trying to eavesdrop, Brad could still overhear their conversation.

"You told me last night that you were sure," Gerald said in a serious undertone. "Are you?"

"Why, of course ah am shuah!" she replied brightly then faltered. "Or nearly so."

"Which is it, Hedy? Do you know? Or are you just stringing me along?"

"Please, darlin', don't be disappointed in me. Ah am tryin' so very hard ... but ah do need time to be shuah that ah am shuah. That is a woman's prerogative."

Brad heard a stifled sob and what sounded like a tearful embrace. He resisted the urge to look over his shoulder.

There was nothing further until Gerald said softly, "I just don't know how much more of this uncertainty I can take. It's breaking my heart."

"Ah understand that, Gerald, but we are bein' rude having this conversation over heah," Hedy rebuked him in soft undertones.

Footsteps approached. Hedy returned, followed

67

closely by Gerald. She was smiling as brightly as she had moments earlier.

"Ah!" she cried. "There you are, you blue-blooded northerner. Did you miss me?"

"Terribly," Brad said.

"I hope Hedy hasn't been telling you any tall tales," Gerald said, glowering. "You shouldn't listen to her stories."

Hedy flopped into a deck chair, her profile high and proud. She took a breath and continued. "Y'all may not know it to look at me, but ah was once the leader of the Young Republican Party. Ah learn from my mistakes, however, and that is one ah won't be making again any time soon."

"Hedy..." Gerald began.

"Now don't shush me, Gerald. It needs to be said." She looked Brad in the eye. "Certain people, sir, want to destroy thousands of low-income housing and ah know why! They are doing it for political gain. And ah have letters to prove it."

Brad glanced at Gerald, waiting to see if he would try to stop her from talking again.

"It's pure and simple. This state is corrupt to the bone. Ah am in possession of a certain incriminating memorandum from a man being groomed to run in the next election. He is a very powerful man and he has connections. Well, ah say connections be damned!"

Gerald put an arm around her shoulder. Was it protective, Brad wondered, or was it a veiled warning? What exactly was Gerald's intention in preventing Hedy from speaking her mind? Whatever the reason, it wasn't working.

"And that is precisely why ah am here. Ah fully intend to spearhead a campaign to convert the empty warehouses along the river into residences for the people who want to come back here to live. Ah have to do it, because they have nothing and no one to turn to."

However impractical-sounding the scheme, Brad was impressed by her zeal.

Just then Gerald's cell phone rang. He answered and spoke in a hushed voice then turned to Hedy. "I have to go. I'll be back later this evening."

He kissed Hedy and left. Hedy waited till he had gone before speaking again.

"Gerald thinks ah do not know it, but ah am well aware that certain forces are tryin' to entice him back to their dark side," she said, sounding like a Star Wars-conspiracy theorist. "Ah hope he will not go over to them."

"You think that was FEMA calling him just now?"

"Ah know it was!" she exclaimed. A spasm of doubt shook her. "On the other hand, ah suppose ah should not be telling him what to do."

"Then I hope he does what his conscience directs him to do."

"Gerald is a good friend," she said. "A very good friend, indeed, but ah worry that he likes me too much."

Yes, he does, Brad thought, and you know it. He likes you far too much for his own good. Especially with that *femme fatale* act you've got going.

"Gerald just doesn't understand that some

things take time. Especially things of an emotional nature." She clenched her fists. "Oh, why can't he just be satisfied and not push for everything right now? On top of that, he's convinced ah'm going to get mahself in trouble for saying the things ah say."

"Perhaps you should exercise caution," Brad suggested.

"Oh, darlin'! Y'all are a pet for listening to me. It's just mah nature. Ah always seem to end up in trouble one way or t'other. It's not like ah need to try!"

She stood and gave him a quick kiss on the cheek then turned and disappeared inside her cabin.

6

Down Dauphine Street and past the railway tracks that cross over at Press Street lies a series of derelict warehouses running corner to corner for several city blocks. Open to the elements, the wind blows through from one side to the other, while birds roost in the rafters and feral cats stalk careless rodents. At one time, the neighbourhood boasted a bustling riverfront where ships from around the world docked to unload their cargo. In that pre-Katrina existence, blue-collar workers toiled in the afternoon sun before drifting over to Po Boys for a mufaletta and a few beers, eventually returning home to their wives and children. Post-Katrina, however, all activity ceased. The wharfs had collapsed and the machines that drove ceaselessly day and night, moving cargo from ship to shore, fell into silence and disuse.

It was here, in this same neighbourhood, that a streetcar made history by becoming the first public transportation vehicle to headline on Broadway. This is the Bywater district of New Orleans, where Desire Street runs alongside Piety, some early city planner's idea of an ecclesiastical joke, no doubt. It's a shabby, ramshackle neighbourhood at the best of times, but it's downright dark and depressing at the worst. This is the sort of neighbourhood where you think twice before venturing alone on its forbidding, tree-lined avenues at night. Whatever lurks in those shadows may be more than a mere mugger. The ghosts of times past are said to linger in Bywater's alleyways. No one would be surprised to see some modern-day Stanley Kowalski trudging drunkenly homeward while an ancient *abuelita* ventures from door to door shopping her "*flores para los muertos.*"

The kindness of strangers notwithstanding, the original Blanche Dubois may well have ended her days on streets very much like these, old, tired, rundown and getting a little flighty with a razor, just one more aging whore with no happy ending in sight.

To a culture vulture like Bradford Fairfax, however, the parish offered a slice of literary fascination, pure and simple. His joy was nearly palpable as he stood beneath the street sign, pointing up like a child sighting Santa on a neighbour's roof at Christmas.

"*Stellaaaaaaa!*" he cried.

"Call me anything you like," Zach beamed. "I'll come running."

"Isn't it amazing to come to New Orleans and find Desire Street?" Brad warbled. "It's like discovering there really is an Oz!"

It was well past sundown, but a faint glow

lingered in the sky. The buildings became more rundown the farther they ventured into the parish. It wasn't long before they located the warehouse hosting the Derelict Disco Spirit Raising Party. It was the only one on the block with lights blazing from its upper windows and music thumping from all of its floors. A spotlight lit up the outside where *You Go GiRL xo!* and *YoU Are BeaUtiful!* had been scripted in giant pink and white lettering below the roofline.

It would have taken a daredevil to paint those letters, Brad noted. In fact, you'd practically have to be hanging upside down from the rooftop to do it. Below, a banner displayed a muscular dancing boy showing off his abs of plutonium. *Reclaim New Orleans!* he commanded from afar. Even here, in one of the most dismal neighbourhoods in a destroyed city, hope—like eccentricity and lust—still sprang eternal.

With Zach at his side, Brad made his way through the doors and up the stairs following the painted arrows and lipstick kisses marking the walls like a trail of salacious breadcrumbs. At the top, they were met by a formidable Amazon in green tights, black halter-top, and an orange wig adorned with glow-in-the-dark hairclips. Two hairy arms were folded across a remorseless bosom.

"Evening, gentlemen. Mah name's Scarlett Onassis-Kennedy Antoinette. Ah'll be yer hostess this evening. Y'all look rich and prosperous, not to mention adorable. Feel free to kiss me at any time. Ah treasure spontaneous displays of overt sexuality and affection."

Brad bowed his head and kissed the glittering ring on Scarlett's gloved hand. "Your majesty," he said.

Scarlett batted her eyelids, creating a minor disturbance of air currents. "Y'all are gonna be in mah will before the evening ends, ah would like to state here and now." She wiped her brow with a hanky. "Just for the record, y'all should know that it has been particularly hard for the poor folks who survived the wrath of Hurricane Katrina to try to stay here to live."

A gloved hand touched her cheek, the very essence of sorrow and grief.

"Many have lost everything, while others are simply unable to return because the price of rent has skyrocketed, to the extent that a poor girl like *moi* is forced to spend more nights on the streets than any working girl should have to, simply in order to make an honest living. Or any kind of living, for that matter. But let's not nitpick."

Scarlett's hands suddenly took flight, in imitation of an airline steward locating emergency exits and washroom stalls. "If y'all are lookin' for someone y'all lost, please feel free to peruse the list of names of former residents on the wall to yer left." The gloves changed direction. "If y'all know of any former residents who have successfully relocated elsewhere—bless their tidy little souls— feel free to add their names and contact numbers to the list on yer right."

She reached up and gave her wig a reassuring pat.

"And how can y'all be of assistance here tonight, y'all must be wonderin'? That's easy." A finger stabbed a sign that read, "DereLict DiscO SpiRit RaiSING ParTy. En-Trance $25. XoX!! AddiTiOnaL ContRibutions !!! WelCome!"

It wasn't hard to figure out who the high-flying sign decorator was, Brad mused.

"I think we can do better than that," he said, pulling out his wallet and handing over a hundred-dollar bill. "For the cause."

The curtsey that rewarded Brad's generosity was as artfully executed as any in the court of the Sun King himself.

"Everlastingly obliged," said Scarlett, fanning herself with the bill before depositing it inside her voluminous cleavage. "For safekeeping only, of course!"

With that, she opened a door and ushered them into a cavernous interior. At the far end, a band plied the airwaves in a blend of rock and Cajun. Derelict it might be, but downcast never. Wooden crates lined the walls and ropes hung in lazy loops from the ceiling. Everything had been hauled up or pushed aside to make room for the glittering party where several hundred men had gathered with infectious gaiety in various states of dress and undress. Mardi Gras masks, muscles, skimpy shorts and peacock feathers were the order of the evening. Only a gay man can turn a derelict warehouse into an opulent extravaganza, thought Brad.

Derek rushed to greet them, a drink in either hand.

"Forgive me, but even here I feel the need to host," he said, handing over the glasses. He winked at Zach "It's bourbon. You've got to start somewhere, darling. Cheers!"

They clinked and drank.

"Looks like a successful party," Brad yelled over the music.

"Yes, so far it's very successful and people are being extremely generous," Derek replied. "Looks like you got here just in time. We've got a surprise coming. Philip's going to make the announcement any moment now."

The band plunged into a crazy quilt of sound coupled to a lurching rhythm: *Eh, maman! Eh, maman! Les haricots sont pas salés.*

Brad's head nodded to the beat. "*Les haricots* is a French phrase that got turned into the Cajun *zydeco*," he said, ever the musicologist.

"Cool," Zach said. "I have no idea what it means, but it's great music."

"*Les haricots sont pas salés* translates as, 'The snap beans ain't salted.' It means we're so poor we can't even afford a bit of salted pork to flavour our beans."

"But not so poor we can't dance. That's what this music is for," Zach said, pulling Brad by the hand and merging into the morass of bodies twisting and gyrating on the open floor.

A pair of scantily clad muscle tykes gyrated at the centre of the action. Brad watched curiously as every few minutes one of them stopped to pose while the other snapped a photo with a cell phone

Brad shook his head. "What's going on? I don't

speak this language."

"Facebook," Zach said. "They're sharing the moment with friends."

"Ah, the younger generation!" Brad exclaimed.

At a signal from one of the organizers, the music died and the dancers came to a halt. Philip leapt up onstage and made his way to the microphone.

"Hello and thanks for coming out tonight," he began. "Y'all will have noticed the lack of expensive décor, which is normally the trademark associated with our festive tribe, but ah feel it is in keeping with the harsh reality of the times and thus in keeping with our theme: *Derelict Disco Spirit Raising Party*. Ah know y'all are here because y'all love this city as much as Derek and ah do, and y'all know it's time for us to work together and do whatever it takes to get back on track. We have sustained a great loss and we have endured much misery, but god willing and with love in our hearts we can turn things around and get our beloved hometown back on its feet again, government or no government!"

Raucous cheers broke out accompanied by raised fists. A spotlight lit the rafters overhead. Philip looked up to see a GI Joe doll descending in a miniature parachute.

"Why, deah me!" he exclaimed. "Whatever can it be?"

He bent and picked up the doll, releasing a slip of paper from the toy soldier's grip.

"Goodness!" he exclaimed. "It is an I.O.U. from the government of the United States for $100 billion dollars and an apology for having treated us so badly. Signed, President George W. Bush."

A resounding chorus of boos filled the hall.

"It seems the Oval Office has not forgot us after all," Philip called out over the fracas. As he turned the paper over, a look of consternation crossed his face. "Oh, merciful heavens," he cried. "Unfortunately, this is written in confederate currency. Oh, deah!"

The crowd roared its approval as Philip tore the note in half and threw the pieces in the air with a shrug. He introduced the next speaker, a city worker charged with heading the restoration campaign. The man thanked the crowd for coming out and began his pitch for the homeless.

Brad turned to Zach. "How are you weathering the bourbon?"

"All right so far."

"Like another?"

"If you think it's safe." He winked.

Brad marched off to the bar. Standing in line, he heard someone speaking in a foreign language. He turned and saw Mr. Nobutsugo and Mr. Sakamoto, the Japanese couple from the Lion's Roar. Derek had invited them, too, it seemed. Then he got a shock. Talking to the pair was a perfect James Dean clone. As he listened, Brad realized he too was speaking Japanese. Dean looked lazily over at Brad, smiled, then bowed to the two Japanese men and made his way to a side exit.

"It really James Dean!" exclaimed Mr. Sakamoto. He nodded excitedly at Brad. "He speak perfect Japanese!"

"Who would have guessed?" Brad said.

No wonder they think of the country as Disneyland, he reflected. To the outside world, America must seem like a giant theme park.

The city worker was just winding up his speech to hearty applause when Brad returned to Zach with a drink. Philip jumped back onstage, his smile radiating across the room.

"Remember, gentlemen—we need y'all to open your hearts as well as your wallets. Every contribution, no matter how small, is welcome." He paused. "And now, ah promise ah will be brief, because even ah am excited by what we are about to see. The moment we have all been waiting for. For your delectable pleasure it is mah great honour to introduce the one and only Harlan Masterson—Gentleman Stripper!"

The slinky music they'd heard at the bar the previous evening wafted through the warehouse. Muscular arms parted the curtains as, once again, Brad's boyhood fascination began to ply his trade.

Harlan performed the same sultry number with the same mesmerizing results. This time, however, as he reached the end of his act the stripper caught Brad's gaze. A smile crossed his face before he vanished behind the curtain. A minute later, he slipped through a side door and into the room, wearing nothing but his silver Speedo. The applause still hung in the air as he grabbed Brad in a mighty grip and crushed him to his chest.

"You old son of a gun, Red!" he roared.

Brad caught Zach's surprised expression over Harlan's shoulder.

"He knows your agent name?" Zach mouthed.

Brad shook his head and shrugged. "No. Hair colour only."

As the pair swayed in each other's arms, Brad was nearly dwarfed by Harlan's massive musculature. Finally, they parted and Brad held Harlan at arm's length.

"It really is you," he said, as though unable to believe it till that very moment. "What are you doing in New Orleans?"

"It was always my ambition to strip my way across the country, one club at a time. And here I am." He looked at Zach. "Who's this little cutie-pie?"

Brad turned to Zach. "This is my partner, Zach."

"You are one lucky son of a gun, Red. This boy is going to be as spectacular as you once he puts a bit of meat on his bones." Harlan regarded Zach. "There's a career in stripping waiting for you, boyo. You could be a rich man. Then again"—he turned back to Brad—"I guess it wouldn't be too smart if you let him take his clothes off in public. Don't let this one get away. He's definitely a keeper."

"I know it," Brad said, a goofy smile spreading over his face as he beamed at his partner. He turned back to Harlan. "By my reckoning, you must have been going at this now for eighteen or nineteen years."

Harlan nodded. "Twenty years this December. By then I'll have danced at every strip club in every city in North America. For a while, I thought

I might head over to Europe, but I think not. I know I'm going to miss it, but it's time to settle down. Forty is the exit door and it's right ahead of me."

Brad gasped. "Forty!"

Harlan laughed. "It's not the end of the world, Red. I've made my fortune and I've had my fame and glory, but there's a little cattle ranch waiting for me in Indiana and me and my lasso are slowly wending our way back home."

"Hope you'll invite us over when you do."

"You bet!" He winked. "Do you still have that T-shirt I gave you?"

Brad gave him another goofy grin. "I sure do."

Zach's gaze travelled back and forth between the two. "Is that by any chance the yellow one that says, 'Moose Lover—Calgary Gay Rodeo'?"

"That's the one, you little sweetheart," Harlan answered.

"It's practically a shrine at our place," Zach informed him. "It has its own shelf in the clothes closet."

By now, the crowd had applauded and stomped themselves into a frenzy. Philip was onstage and calling for Harlan to return for an encore.

"I'm here for a week," Harlan said. "I'm staying at the old Olivier House. Great place. Creaky. Lotta ghosts. We should get together for old times' sakes." He looked over at Zach. "Nothing to worry about, angel face. I'm talking drinks, but if you care to join us"—he winked—"we could change the menu to suit you."

Suddenly he was gone, leaping back onstage.

81

The spotlight flared and the crowd settled in as Harlan began one last number. When he finished, he gave Brad a quick salute before disappearing into the wings. The band returned and the crowd resumed its blissful enjoyment of the evening. All was well in the gayest of gay worlds.

By midnight, Brad was ready to head back to the inn. His third bourbon had nearly done him in. Zach had stopped after the second, but agreed the effect was powerful.

As they were leaving, Brad waved goodbye to Derek and Philip. The Japanese couple had already left. Off in a far corner a dashing young man in a tuxedo, his hair neatly coiffed, flashed robin's egg-blue eyes across the room. Sometimes you *can* dress them up and take them out, Brad thought. The crowd swirled around him and Quint was suddenly gone.

Outside, a light rain fell as Brad and Zach sauntered homeward. Brad's head was spinning from the bourbon as they headed up Dauphine Street, their footsteps echoing behind them.

Up ahead, a bonfire blazed in an abandoned parking lot. Cries hung in the air. The silhouettes of near-naked young men could be seen leaping over the flames. Someone smashed a bottle on the hood of a car, while others banged with sticks on empty crates. It could have been a party or it could have been a looting spree. If nothing else, it confirmed that New Orleans was in the hands of punks and petty criminals. There was no sense in interfering. Apart from the wanton destruction, no one seemed in danger. Brad and Zach trooped noiselessly past.

On reaching the Lion's Roar, all was silent. They let themselves in and headed down the path along the main building. A single light gleamed over the entrance to the courtyard. As they emerged by the pool, the dogs came out to greet them, wagging tails and glowing green in the sheen cast by the underwater lights. Serenity ruled the waves. Heads were patted and the dogs trotted off obediently.

They had just reached their cabin when a scream pierced the night air.

7

The scream echoed around the courtyard and rippled over the pool. As one, Brad and Zach whirled and dashed back down the walk. They found themselves outside Hedy's cabin just as a second scream erupted from within. The door opened at Brad's touch. Hedy lay crumpled on the floor. Across the room, curtains wavered over the sill.

"Stay with her!" Brad shouted, racing to the window.

He hoisted himself through the gap and landed with a thud in the garden. Someone was scurrying in the shrubbery up ahead. Brad followed, brushing aside palm fronds and giant salvia leaves.

The sound of an engine starting caught his ear. Tires screeched as a phantom vehicle peeled away from the curb, a blur in the night. Brad propelled himself forward, nearly reaching it as the car zoomed off down the street. It was a black Dodge Challenger escaped from some 70s time-warp.

Headlights snapped on. He was just able to glimpse the license plate as it raced around a corner and vanished from sight. Brad strained his ears until he couldn't hear it any more. Cicadas ruled the still night air. The parish seemed deserted.

He retraced his steps to where the car had been parked. The gutters were filled with mud from the recent rains. If he returned with a flashlight, he might find a set of tracks. Right now, though, he needed to get back to the inn.

The dogs were gathered outside Hedy's door, whining and scratching to be let in. Zach opened to his knock. Hedy sat on the floor, absent-mindedly petting the white cat in her lap. She looked up as Brad entered.

"Thank you," she said. "Y'all are true heroes. Both of you."

"Can you tell us what happened?" Brad asked.

She put a hand to her face. "Ah woke up and he was standing right beside my bed. Ah was too terrified to move. Ah thought he was going to rape me."

"Did you recognize him?" Brad asked.

Hedy shook her head. "Ah never saw him before in mah life."

"Can you describe him?"

"He was hideous. Frightful. He had a long, ghoulish face. One side of his head was shaved down to nothing. Just the one side." Hedy shivered.

With a jolt, Brad recalled the man who had been observing him and Zach at the restaurant the previous evening.

"Is that how he got in?" Brad asked, nodding to the window.

"Ah ... ah'm not sure," Hedy replied. "Ah was asleep."

Brad knelt and examined the door frame. There was no sign of a forced entry.

"Was it locked when you went to bed?" he asked.

Hedy shrugged. "Ah can't say, darling. It might have been. Ah never notice these things."

Brad resisted an urge to tell her off for being so careless. Instead, he said, "Do you have any idea why someone would break into your room?"

Hedy shook her head, but her response wasn't all that convincing.

"Could he have been after your jewellery?" Brad asked, eyeing a string of pearls draped casually over the bedside table.

Hedy looked over. She picked up the necklace and twirled it around a finger.

"Not likely, darlin', but if he did then he's welcome to it. None of it's real. If they were, ah would have pawned them to help someone in need." She turned her gaze to meet Brad's. "He may have been after the letters. The ones ah told you about."

"From the powerful man you mentioned."

"Yes," Hedy said quietly.

She went to the dresser and pulled open the top drawer, removing a half-empty Bourbon bottle and setting it upright on the dresser. Several pill bottles joined it, along with a scarf and a pair of nylons. Next, she scooped out a pile of letters tied in a pink ribbon.

"The others are safe on my laptop," she said,

though Bradford had doubts about her use of the adjective "safe."

"Do you feel up to talking about why you had to run away with these letters?"

Hedy nodded. "It's because ah found out what's been going on. And what ah learned has shocked me. The thing is, they don't want people to return here. Specifically the African-Americans."

"Who doesn't want people to return?"

"Politicians, mostly. Ah'm not naïve about any of this. No one is ever going to come out and say that African-Americans are not welcome back in their homes, but that is the truth of it. That's why we are facing the wholesale demolition of thousands of low-income apartment units."

"I may be a little slow, but I still don't understand," said Bradford.

"They're trying to change the voting population by changing the demographics," Zach said.

"That's right, darling," Hedy pronounced with a meaningful look. "Louisiana is a so-called 'pink' state. We are one that runs red and blue—sometimes Republican and sometimes Democrat. It's the African-Americans who vote Democrat in Louisiana. The tipping point for the Louisiana Democratic Party is this city right heah."

Brad nodded. "I'm beginning to see."

Hedy continued. "After the hurricane, when all those people were gathered under the roof of the Superdome, I thought to myself: the Democratic majority of Louisiana is asleep inside the Superdome. That's when I woke up to the reality of what was going on. And that's why certain

87

political figures are trying to make sure they don't return to N'Orleans. They thought no one would figure it out, but I've been wising people up. That's why they all hate me."

"Who hates you?" Brad asked.

"That very powerful gentleman ah spoke of, for one. He wrote a note to mah former boss saying the decent people of Louisiana had been unable to clean up the city's filth, but that God had finally done so with His handiwork. 'And now it's time for us to continue God's handiwork,' he said." Her eyes narrowed. "Ah believe he would very much like to have that letter back so he could destroy it."

"So what you're saying is, you think someone broke in to steal the letters. Perhaps someone sent by this powerful man," Brad pressed.

"It could be."

"Is it also possible the Democrats want to the letters to embarrass the Republicans?" Zach asked.

"Very likely, darling. They would no doubt be valuable to certain people for the embarrassment they could cause, though ah'm not sure any of it is going to benefit the good people of N'Orleans."

"From what I understand," Brad said, "the Republicans pride themselves on their history of breaking and entering, while the Democrats prefer sex scandals."

"Ah'd say that's a pretty fair assessment."

"We'll need to report this to the police," Brad said.

"No, darling!" Hedy looked alarmed. "Please don't tell anyone."

Brad looked sharply at her. "Why?"

"Because ... because..." Hedy looked away.

"Is it because of this very powerful gentleman you keep mentioning?"

"Yes."

"Who is he?"

Hedy turned slowly to meet Bradford's gaze. "He is the Republican party's up-and-coming senatorial candidate for the state of Louisiana. He is also mah husband."

"I'm beginning to see," Brad said. "You think your husband is behind the break-in?"

Hedy shrugged. "It's possible. On the other hand, ah suppose he could simply be looking for evidence of mah infidelity. Which he will not find, however." She looked up defiantly. "The truth is, ah have not been unfaithful to mah husband. Gerald has been a true gentleman to wait for me to make up mah mind. He must continue to wait, however, because ah won't have it any other way."

Voices reached them from the alley. The dogs rushed off to greet Philip and Derek returning from the party. When Brad told them what had happened, they were shaken to learn that such a thing had occurred on their property.

"Ah'm terribly sorry, gentlemen," Hedy offered. "This will teach me to be more sensible. Ah will remember to lock mah door and latch mah window next time."

Against their better judgement, Derek and Philip agreed not to notify the police, reluctantly acknowledging that the New Orleans Police force in its present state was not always to be trusted. Hedy declined the offer of a room inside the inn, but accepted another cabin closer to the main house. It was nearly three AM by the time things calmed down.

After the others had gone to bed, Brad took Zach to where the getaway car had been parked. He shone a flashlight on the ground, but the mud was too watery to have left tire marks. They searched further, but there was nothing that looked like it would be of any help. At least Brad had the car make and license number.

A call to Grace ensued. Brad explained what had happened and relayed the pertinent information.

"How much do you know about this girl?" Grace asked, her voice sounding as though she'd just smoked a really good cigar.

"The Republicans were training her to be a lobbyist, apparently, but when it came to the crunch she couldn't decide whose side she was on. It also sounds like someone in the Democratic Party might be interested in what she has to offer, but I gather Hedy doesn't have much faith that either side will restore her hometown now."

"And sadly, there is no third side," Grace said. "Those parties are about two degrees apart in their policies. That's one of the funny things about American politics. It's not really about right or wrong or even which side you're on, it's about winning at any cost."

Brad smiled as his boss launched into her diatribe.

"You may recall from your history books that President Abraham Lincoln was renowned for emancipating the slaves, causing a great uproar with the southern half of the US, who were largely dependent on slave labour. What people conveniently overlook now is that Mr. Lincoln was president of the Republican Party—the *liberal* Yankee party, to be precise, and not the Democrats, who back then were the *conservative* southern good old boys."

"I never thought about that," Brad said.

"Nobody does. But somewhere along the way the Republicans and the Democrats simply switched sides. Now look which way the wind blows. As I say, it doesn't matter in the least which side you're on, so don't even try to understand US politics. It will scramble your brains. It's all about winning, which is why lobbying is such a major part of the strategy. Of course, there are no longer black slaves in the US, just illegal immigrants who do the same work about as cheaply. Somebody's always at the top of the wheel trying to keep somebody else at the bottom."

She had a point, Brad thought. Several, in fact.

"And what of the husband?" Grace asked. "He sounds like a shady character to me. We need to find out how much influence he really has."

"I'll try to find out more in the morning," Brad said, stifling a yawn. "Hedy was pretty exhausted by the ordeal, so we let her get to sleep. From what I can tell, she seems to be a functional alcoholic, or bordering on one. Derek said she barely drank when he met her a year ago, but she drinks pretty much non-stop now."

Grace *tsked*.

"As for the boyfriend," Brad went on, "Gerald seems to be genuinely in love with her, but I suspect it's not mutual. I think he's trying to save her from herself. There's a permanent cloud over her head. She seems to enjoy playing the tragic heroine. Derek's afraid she's going to ruin him."

"I'm sure you don't need a lecture on Southern Belles," Grace said. "Just be wary of whatever she says. You should be thankful you're gay."

"I am every day of my life," Brad said, glancing over at Zach. "Very thankful."

"Then let's hope nothing comes along to change it," Grace said ominously, ending things on her usual dour note.

8

The sun cast its warming beams through the curtains and over the sill. An exhausted Zach lay snoring on his side. They'd been up till four AM, but Brad couldn't sleep. He slipped out to the courtyard where the dogs were racing madly about, menacing invisible prey and slinking around the pool.

He'd been there a few minutes when a panicked-looking Gerald arrived.

"She's all right," Brad called out, before he could speak. "Philip and Derek moved her to cabin number eight, over by the main building."

Gerald nodded his thanks then went to Hedy's room and knocked. The door opened and he slipped inside. Brad heard murmuring voices. Hedy seemed to be consoling Gerald, beseeching him not to be afraid for her.

The clanking of a pail alerted Brad to Quint's arrival. The boy was dressed only in cut-off shorts. Brad noticed the "V" tattooed above his right collarbone. With his long, lean torso and the profile of a minor Roman god, he was exquisite to look at. As he advanced, his hips moved rhythmically from side to side. A trail of blonde hair ran from his pectorals down to his navel and disappeared inside his shorts. He was as adorable as a six-month-old puppy.

The boy began his rounds, sloshing his pail along the paths. Brad watched curiously, recalling his appearance at the party the night before. Having mopped the tiles, Quint picked up a net and headed for the pool. He knelt and pulled a drowned butterfly from the water's surface. A tear rolled down his cheek.

He's young, Brad thought. But not so young as to cry over every living thing that dies.

"It's sad, Quint, but life goes on..."

The boy stood sheltering the dead insect in his palm. "Sometimes."

"Yes, you're right—sometimes, but not always. Not for everyone. We're the lucky ones." He smiled at the boy. "How old are you, Quint?"

"Last week ah was eighteen. This week ah'm nineteen."

An odd way of putting it, Brad thought. "You're a birthday boy then. Happy birthday!"

"Thank you," Quint said dolefully, as though not at all sure it was an occasion for congratulations.

"How'd you enjoy the party last night?"

Quint blinked in confusion. "Party?"

Brad nodded. "The disco warehouse party. Did you enjoy it?"

"No, ah didn't enjoy a party," the boy replied, shaking his head.

"That was you, right? Wearing a tuxedo?"

94

He frowned. "A tuxedo?"

"At the party. I saw you wearing a tuxedo. You looked quite snazzy."

He shook his head. "No, Mr. Bradford. Quint doesn't go to parties."

Brad shook his head. Had he been mistaken? He was sure it had seen him. Just then the bell rang at the front gate. A fearful look crossed Quint's face. The boy stood rooted to the spot. The bell rang a second time. Quint slipped quietly behind a hedge. Brad was about to answer when Derek came out of the inn and headed down the walk. The Englishman soon returned carrying a package and some letters.

"Good morning, Bradford! Juice and biscuits are coming right up," he said, heading back inside with the mail.

A few minutes later he returned with a tray of glasses, a large pitcher and a steaming plate of hushpuppies.

"Sorry we're a bit late this morning. Coffee will be ready in a minute." He placed the tray on the table. "Or would you prefer tea?"

"Coffee's good," Brad said. "I need something strong after last night."

Derek reached for his hip flask. Brad shook his head.

"Not that strong," he said.

"Yes, it was quite a shock," Derek agreed. "Even Philip needed a shot of bourbon to get to sleep afterwards. I'm still not sure we made the right choice in not calling the police, but with the state of things in this town you can never tell whether the police are going to do something for you or to you."

"I hear you," Brad said. "I related the incident to the agency, you'll be glad to know."

Derek nodded quickly. "Yes, I'm grateful to hear it."

"Hi, Derek!" Quint called out from behind the shrubbery.

"Hello, you beautiful young man," Derek called back. "Are you hiding from the postman? He's gone now." He turned apologetically to Brad. "He's a bit odd, I know. I hope one day he gets back to normal."

"I thought I saw him at the party last night," Brad said quietly.

"Really?" Derek laughed and shook his head. "Impossible. Not Quint. He hasn't once left the property here, as far as I know. Not since the day we brought him back from the hospital."

"Not once?"

Derek smiled a wry smile. "I know—it's odd. What's a beauty like that doing hiding himself here at the inn?

"Do you think it's a phobia?" Brad asked.

Derek nodded. "That's what Philip and I believe. We invite him to come with us in the car to get supplies or just for a drive, but he never accepts. He was pretty messed up when he landed on our doorstep. I suspect he's grown phobic about being beaten again. We've asked him to see a therapist, but of course he won't leave the grounds and we haven't found anyone willing to come here and see him. Maybe when things get back to normal..."

"He can't live on your grounds forever, as beautiful as they are," Brad said, eyeing the garden.

"I agree, but I'm not sure what to do about it." Derek looked over at Quint, calling the boy's name.

"Howdy, Derek!" He came up to them, smiling.

"Quint, you're doing a great job here. Would you like to go for a ride downtown later on for some ice cream?"

The boy froze. "Downtown?"

"Sure. I'll buy you any flavour you want."

"Quint doesn't want any flavours, Derek," he said.

"Are you sure? We'll only be gone an hour or so."

He shook his head vigorously. "Take care!"

Derek sighed. "Quint, are you afraid to leave the inn?"

"Take care, Derek," the boy said fearfully.

"You know I won't let anyone hurt you. You trust me to look after you, don't you?"

Quint nodded. Derek held out his hand. Quint slowly reached out and took it.

"I want you to come with me..."

Quint dug his heels into the ground. "Where?"

"Just to the gate, Quint. I promise not to make you go any farther, if you don't want to. Will you trust me?"

Brad watched as they inched toward the front gate and stopped in front of it. Derek let go of Quint's hand and slowly swung the gate open onto the street. Quint froze again.

Derek turned to the boy. "It's the whole wide world out there, Quint."

The boy's eyes were wide and shining with fear. "Ah know. It's big."

"Don't you want any part of it?"

Quint shook his head. "Dog said we're not supposed to leave the garden."

As he watched, Brad grew more and more curious.

"Are you afraid of what's out there, Quint?" Derek asked.

"Dog is out there!" Quint shivered. He stood paralyzed. "Take care!"

A woman passing on the sidewalk stopped to regard the curious sight of a boy unable to step beyond an invisible boundary.

"Chester?" she called out tentatively.

Derek looked up at the woman, but Quint's gaze remained fixed on the invisible line at his feet.

"Chester, it's me. Lucy Kalman," the woman persisted.

Quint looked right past her as though she didn't exist.

"Chester Morgenstern? Don't you know me?"

"Do you know this young man?" Derek asked.

She nodded vigorously. "Yes, but we thought he was..." Her voice trailed off. "We thought he was *lost* after the storm. It is you, isn't it Chester?"

Quint looked at her and shook his head. "Mah name is Quint," he said.

The woman appeared mystified. Something about Quint's expression seemed to frighten her.

"I'm sorry," she said, backing away. "I mistook you for a former neighbour." Her eyes sought out the others. "We've been so worried. My apologies."

"Wait," Derek said.

He stepped through the gate and spoke quietly to her for a moment then returned. The woman walked away, turning once to look back at Quint with a bewildered expression.

Derek closed the gate and regarded Quint. "She certainly seemed to think she knew you," he said. "Do you know a Chester Morgenstern?"

Quint shook his head. "No. Ah'm Quint," he insisted patiently, as though that settled the matter.

Brad watched him slip off to the far end of the grounds and disappear behind the shrubbery.

"That was strange." Derek turned to Brad with a sober expression. "She said Quint looks exactly like her former neighbour, the son of a local Baptist preacher named Septimus Morgenstern. Septimus has a reputation for being anti-everything the Bible says you're supposed to be against. Even in this tolerant city, we still have a few of the fanatical types."

"Maybe Quint's running away from a bad home life," Brad suggested. "This might be his way out."

"Could be," Derek said. He glanced over his shoulder where Quint had begun to sweep the walk. "It's just odd. It makes me think of the friend who passed me by as though he didn't know who I was."

A voice boomed out. "Morning, y'all!"

Philip stood at the doorway of the inn with a

tray of coffee, beaming out at the world.

"Good morning," Brad replied.

"Hey, Philip!" Quint called out, waving from behind a bush.

"Hello, you ray of sunshine!" Philip called back.

Derek turned to Brad and said quietly, "In any case, Quint's a great worker and Philip and I both love him. Whatever he wants his story to be is fine with us."

The front bell rang again.

"Ah'll get it," Philip said.

He opened the gate to a tall, dark-featured man with chiselled good looks.

"Good morning. Can ah help you?" Philip asked.

"I'm looking for my wife," the man said.

"Who would that be, sir?"

"Her name is Hedy Pritchard. I don't know what fool name she calls herself here."

Philip hesitated. "There is a Hedy staying with us. Ah'll see if she's in. Please wait heah." He closed the gate without letting the man in.

"Tell her that her husband is here," the man called after him.

Philip went up to Hedy's cottage and knocked. She opened it with a radiant smile.

"Yes, darling?"

"There's a man at the front gate who says he's your husband."

Her smile vanished. "Is he a tall, handsome man with the black heart of a villain?"

"That's him," Philip agreed.

"Well, then ah guess it must be a fact. Ah shall go and speak to the gentleman in question."

Gerald appeared in the doorway behind her. Hedy's look made it clear he was not to accompany her. She went to the gate and gazed unhappily at the man on the other side. Brad saw her shake her head once or twice, with growing agitation on the husband's part. The voices grew loud.

"Ah just can't, Tyrone. Ah'm sorry."

"Then why did you call me last night?" Hedy's husband demanded.

Two of the dogs trotted up and stood beside Hedy, prepared to defend her.

"Ah was afraid! He came right into my room and ah didn't know who else to call. You know he's not a nice man."

"And you think I sent him?"

"Ah thought you might have done."

"Well, in that case, I suggest that if he returns you give him what he wants and he'll go away."

One of the dogs growled.

"You know ah cain't do that, Tyrone."

"Then I guess you'll have to take your chances."

The man glanced at the group seated around the patio and lowered his voice again. Brad's ears were burning. Clearly, both Hedy and her husband knew the man who broke into her room, despite Hedy's vehement denial the previous night.

Unable to restrain himself, Gerald walked boldly down the laneway and stood beside Hedy, placing a hand firmly on her shoulder.

"Everything all right, Hedy?" he asked.

"Yes, Gerald."

Tyrone regarded him with narrowed eyes.

"This is what you left me for?" he spat out with contempt.

"Hedy left you because you were an abusive bastard," Gerald exploded. "You need to leave her alone. She doesn't ever want to see you again!"

"Well, you'll have to take that up with Hedy," Tyrone snarled, as though she weren't there. "Because when she had a problem last night, you, sir, were not the one she called."

Gerald shot her an accusing look.

"Ah called because ah was in mortal danger!" Hedy cried.

Gerald turned to Tyrone, pushing out his chest. "Hedy doesn't need you anymore. Leave here and don't come back. We don't want to see your face again."

It was all so *Gone with the Wind*, Brad thought. Perhaps a duel would ensue between the pair. These people behaved as though they were living a century-and-a-half earlier. Then again, the flooding of New Orleans during Hurricane Katrina might not be so very different from the burning of Atlanta during the Civil War if you happened to live in either of those respective cities at the time.

"Hedy!" Tyrone called.

"Please leave, Tyrone."

"I will be back. Clearly you don't know what's good for you."

With that, he turned and walked away.

Gerald stormed up the walk, dragging Hedy along behind him.

"Why did you ask him here?" he demanded. "I thought you said you were through with him!"

"Ah didn't ask him to come here, Gerald. Maybe ah did say ah was through with him, but he just—"

"How did he find out where you were?" Gerald demanded. "I thought the whole point of being here was to hide from him."

"Ah know, Gerald, but ah must have let it slip last night when ah was so terrified!"

"When you were so drunk, you mean!" Gerald stopped and turned to her. "You made me swear to protect you from him, and now I find out you called him here. Why can't you make up your mind, Hedy?"

"Ah am trying, Gerald, but ah cain't just forget him!" she wailed. "Please try to be patient!"

Gerald released her arm. "Damn it all, Hedy! I've run out of patience."

"Please!" Hedy said, gripping his shirtsleeves as though he were the last train leaving a country about to be overrun by invading forces. "Please, Gerald darling. Ah need you, honey!"

As much as Brad disliked Hedy's *femme fatale* routine, he felt sorry for her. Even Scarlett O'Hara could have stood on her own without that simpering goody-goody Rhett Butler, he thought.

Exasperated, Gerald turned and left. The gate slammed behind him. Even without the "Frankly, my dear, I don't give a damn" line, it was an exit fit for a drama queen of any sex.

With the excitement over, Philip and Derek slipped discreetly back inside the inn.

Hedy continued to stare at the gate, stamping her foot in annoyance. "Men!" she cried then turned to find Brad watching her. "Perhaps ah had better become a nun." She frowned. "Are there Baptist nuns?"

Brad shrugged. "That I don't know. What will you do now?"

"Why, ah will just continue on with mah project of helping the poor and the needy. There is so much that needs to be done. Ah can't stand to see all this suffering."

With a sigh, she stepped over to the table and picked up a glass of juice. Brad watched as she slipped a small bottle from her pocket and poured herself a consolatory drink with a particularly volatile bourbon-to-juice ratio.

Brad nodded. "It's all well and good to care about other people, Hedy, but if you don't mind my saying so, it looks like you've got a few issues of your own. You need to decide what to do about your husband and then let Gerald know whether you want him in your life or not. I think he deserves that much, at least."

Hedy gave him her most beguiling smile. "Thank you, darling. Ah'm overwhelmed by your concern."

She sipped from her glass, twirling it in her fingers where it reflected the light. "Such beautiful, sad colours..." she murmured and headed back to her cabin.

Once she was gone, Brad looked over to the garden to see Quint peering out from behind a palm. He waved and the boy waved back.

"It's safe to come out now," Brad called.

9

An hour later, Zach emerged from the cabin stretching and yawning. Brad looked up from his newspaper and smiled. "Good morning," he called out.

"Good morning."

Just then Derek arrived with a tray of tantalizing biscuits. Zach poured a glass of juice and dug in.

"Wow," he said, after Brad filled him in on the recent drama. "This place is non-stop excitement."

Brad had just turned back to his newspaper when the Japanese couple emerged from their room. They took a cautious look around, as though emerging from a shelter after a storm.

"Coast is clear?" asked Mr. Nobutsugo.

"It's all good," Brad informed them.

Mr. Sakamoto stretched his arms overhead and looked up at the sky. "Beautiful sky," he said, smiling cheerfully. "This what we call a penis day."

Startled, Brad cast his gaze upward. "Really?" he asked. He could discern no particular reason for Mr. Sakamoto's declaring the day to be phallic.

Then again, the two were on their honeymoon. Sex on the brain, he decided, casting his eyes back to his paper, embarrassed by the naiveté of foreigners.

Zach looked over with a bemused grin. "I think Mr. Sakamoto is saying this is what the Japanese refer to as a 'happiness' day."

"Yes," Mr. Sakamoto agreed, smiling broadly. "All want a penis. Very important."

Brad took this in stride. "You're absolutely right. We all do," he said agreeably. "How are you enjoying your stay in New Orleans?"

The two men bowed slightly. "Yes, very much for thank you," said Mr. Nobutsugo.

Brad returned the gesture. "Philip mentioned you were beekeepers."

The Japanese couple looked at one another in confusion.

"He said you were here to find some bees," Brad explained.

A light of recognition went on. They smiled effusively. "Ah, yes. We want to find some bees! Very good."

"Philip said you want to film them," Brad told them.

They nodded. "Yes. We want flim some bees."

The couple finished their coffee and went off on their quest.

Brad and Zach readied themselves for another tour of the city, this time on foot, hoping to investigate Hedy's claim about the destruction of low-income housing.

That afternoon they toured some of the sites

designated for demolition by FEMA. The people they encountered were only too happy to tell their tales of woe. Word on the street was very much in accord with Hedy's contention that the reconstruction was being done to suit the haves at the expense of the have nots, while changing the balance of voting in favour of the Republicans. Although many were disturbed by the overall prospect, housing was obviously a far more immediate concern.

On the outskirts of the Ninth Ward, they came across a blind street singer, his clothes as ragged as his voice. "Ain't nobody got no money, while the misery just grows and grows..." seemed to be the extent of his doleful lament.

"Amen to that, brother," Brad called out, dropping some coins into the man's hat.

A quick online search the previous evening had revealed the astonishing statistic that more than 60,000 New Orleans residents remained homeless since returning to the city. Meanwhile, the average rent had more than doubled in the time they were gone. It was a sobering fact, but Agent Red wasn't convinced there was anything he and Agent Kong could do other than report back on the tales of corruption and leave it in the hands of others more powerful and better situated to change things. Still, a very obvious question nagged at the back of his brain: Why were they in New Orleans? Grace had said the answer was somewhere out there on the streets. No doubt it promised to be a curious one.

It was late afternoon by the time they finished

their walk. They had just started back to the inn when they passed a crowd of people lined up outside a movie house. Brad saw a boyish figure in jeans and T-shirt slip inside the theatre. Once again, he was sure he'd just seen Quint wandering about far from the inn.

"Did you see that?" Brad asked, but Zach's attention had been elsewhere.

"See what?"

"I could have sworn I saw Quint duck inside this movie theatre. But how could it be, if he never leaves the inn?"

A man in tattered clothing, his hair covered in slime and pieces of what looked like raw flesh sliding off his face, lurched up to the pair and held out a flyer.

"Check it out, dudes. Big Zombie fest on tonight."

Brad looked up at the theatre marquee: ZOMBIE FILM FESTIVAL. Tonight: *Lavender Zombies of San Francisco* on a double bill with *Zombies Vs. George W Bush.*

"All right!" Zach exclaimed. "I heard about this one. Bush gets his comeuppance at long last."

"Well, I suppose there's one way to find out if Quint is inside," Brad said, heading for the box office.

The lights were just going down as they entered the theatre. There was no time to look for Quint. After stumbling over many pairs of feet, Brad and Zach sat near the back of a very full house, claiming two of the last available seats. The opening feature proved to be a musical about a band of gay zombies who lived on Alcatraz by day and roamed the streets of San Francisco by night. Naturally, it had an unapologetically happy ending with a finale worthy of Busby Berkeley. The audience went mad.

At the film's end, the lights came up. Near the front, Brad spied a figure that might have been Quint talking to two other men. With a start, Brad recognized the Japanese couple from the Lion's Roar. Before he could make his way over, however, the Quint look-a-like nodded and headed for the exit. Brad pushed through the crowd to the front of the theatre.

"Hello there!" he called out.

The couple turned and smiled on seeing him. "Mr. Bradford. You like some bees too!"

Brad looked at them in confusion. Suddenly it dawned on him: "Oh, yes. Some bees," he said, nodding. "Yes, I like zombies. This is what you came to America to find?" he asked, recalling the Japanese obsession for horror flics.

"Yes!" they nodded enthusiastically. "We love it!"

Brad looked toward the exit door. "Am I wrong or was that Quint you were talking to?"

The two looked at one another and conferred quickly in Japanese. Mr. Sakamoto turned to Brad and shook his head. "Oh, no," he said in a sombre tone. "That defrinitely not Quint."

Brad wondered if he'd been mistaken or if the pair was lying. "I could have sworn..." he began, as another familiar face caught his eye over Mr. Sakamoto's shoulder. There in the flesh—or something very much like it—stood Montgomery Clift, looking alive and decidedly young, as though he'd come back to life at the age of twenty-four.

"Isn't that—?" he began.

The Japanese couple laughed. "No!" they cried in tandem.

"Are you sure?" Brad said, wondering at the man's uncanny resemblance to the dead movie star.

"We thought so too," said Mr. Sakamoto. "We ask him for autograph, but he speak only Polish! He not Crift Montgromery. Just actor."

They broke into peals of laughter. At that moment, the lights dimmed. Bradford crawled back over the rows of feet to rejoin Zach, happily munching popcorn and waiting to see George W. Bush get his comeuppance. Cheers greeted the opening credits. The film would be especially relevant to a New Orleans audience, Brad knew.

It was a long and gory movie with no happy ending, beginning or even middle. After the final credits, Brad staggered out into the night feeling a little green. An elated Zach followed at his heels.

"Didn't you just love it when Condoleezza Rice cut off Bush's head with the samurai sword to keep him from turning the US into a zombie-controlled state? That was so cool!" Zach enthused. "Too bad it's just a movie."

"I suppose," Brad said, taking a breath and leaning against a wall. "I guess I don't share the fascination for zombie films. All that gore."

"That was the best part!" Zach exclaimed.

"For the record, Agent Kong, I'd prefer a Marx

Brothers retrospective next time."

"Deal," said Zach.

"So what's the story on zombies?" Brad asked as they walked along the street. "Do they really exist?"

"Well, sort of yes but no not really," Zach said. "As you know, zombies are associated with Voodoo, which New Orleans is famous for. In reality, it's Haitian Voodoo that gave us zombies. But the walking undead-type of zombies—that is, zombies brought back to life from the remains of the dead—are just a myth, like vampires."

"Yeesh! Don't tell Anne Rice that."

"I would never try to make an author face facts." Zach shrugged. "On the other hand, evidence suggests that it's possible to induce a zombie-like state in humans by using a combination of drugs and mind control. They're not really dead, of course, just in a semi-conscious state. They say that really devious practitioners bury their victims after drugging them and then dig them up later to convince people they've been brought back from the dead."

At that moment, a street singer who might have been a brother to the previous one in both looks and musical tastes walked up to them. "Times is bad, friends, times is bad," he moaned while thwacking his guitar. "The living is ugly and the dead be all sad." Brad tossed him a coin.

After the singer passed by, Zach continued. "Louisiana Voodoo is different from its Haitian cousin in other ways as well. While the Haitians gave us zombies and Voodoo dolls, Louisiana Voodoo gave us the *gris-gris*—or medicine amulet—as well as Voodoo queens like Marie Laveau. For the most part, Louisiana Voodoo is benevolent. Marie Laveau worked as an intercedent on behalf of the poor, the hungry and the sick."

"Is this a lecture? Should I take notes?"

"Nah. I'll remember it for you. Anyway, true Voodoo is considered an 'ecstatic' religion, so sex is cool."

"Sounds progressive," Brad said.

"Haitians believe that sexual orientation is something God determines as part of an individual's make-up."

"Well, there's one religion that has its head screwed on straight ... er, right. Someone should inform all the other religious fanatics around the world."

Zach smiled. "And get this—as gay men we fall under the protection of the spirit Erzulie Freda, also known as the Black Madonna. Erzulie is the goddess of love, beauty, jewellery, dancing, luxury, and flowers."

"That about covers it," Brad nodded. "Cologne, maybe. And interior design. Any idea which drugs are used to turn people into zombies?"

"It's a potent brew made of poison extracted from the puffer, also known as the blowfish."

"The kind they serve in Japanese restaurants?"

"Yes, the same. The process is excruciatingly exacting. You have to be licensed to serve blowfish. Quite a few people die every year eating puffers, which are the second-most poisonous vertebrate in the world."

"I don't even want to know what the first one

is," Brad said.

"The Golden Dart Frog, also known as *Phyllobates terribilis.*"

"Where do you come up with this stuff?" Brad asked as they continued toward the Marigny.

"*The New Orleans Guide for Tourists.* It's in our room next to the phone."

"So can this poison brew make a man do something he normally wouldn't do or maybe something totally antithetical to his nature?"

"Yes and no," Zach said.

"Are there no simple answers to these things?"

"Well, yes..."

"... and no," Brad chimed in. "Got it."

"It depends on your belief system," Zach continued. "There's a type of Voodoo practitioner called the bokor who are said to 'practice with both hands,' meaning they practice both dark magic as well as the more benevolent kind. They're the ones who supposedly created zombies."

"I see."

"Once the victim is drugged, the bokor has to continuously administer deliriants like datura to keep the victim in a dreamlike state. That way, they're highly suggestible. It's pretty much like being under mind control."

"Sounds like one party I could do without," Brad said.

They had just reached the inn when Brad's cell phone rang. It was Grace. She'd received word on the licence plate.

"The license checks out, Red, but the car make doesn't. Looks like the plate was lifted from a

113

former police car destroyed in the flooding."

"That's ironic," Brad said. "I wonder who did the lifting. It could have been a former police officer."

"An interesting and entirely plausible suggestion," Grace replied.

"From what we've seen of the sorry state of things around here, anything is possible."

"The Challenger lead isn't much help either," she continued. "An oldie but goodie. However, there are too many classic car aficionados to narrow it down quickly."

"Hmmm..."

Grace continued. "On the other hand, we managed to look into Hedy's former boss as well as her husband. There's probably a lot that goes on down there without the rest of the state's knowledge, but I daresay there's little that passes the attention of those two gentlemen. Tyrone Pritchard is a strong contender for the Louisiana legislature. He's Big News, as they say. And Hedy's former boss is his biggest backer."

"Anything we should be doing about either of them?" Brad said, with a glance at Zach.

"Not just at present. The other interesting tag of information I came across is that your young lady seems to have an FBI dossier."

"Meaning she is being investigated?"

"That is highly probable. I haven't managed to get my hands on it—yet. But the fact that it exists is worth taking note of."

As per usual with Grace, the call ended abruptly. Brad updated Zach on the findings. Up ahead, beside the pool, Gerald sat with his head nodding onto his chest. He jerked awake at their approach.

"Hedy?"

"No," Brad said. "Did she stand you up?"

"No need. I can stand up on my own." The bear of a man stood tipsily, not exactly proving his point.

Brad ignored his drunkenness. "No, I meant did she make arrangements to meet you here..."

"Wha...? What arrangements?"

Brad decided not to bother explaining.

"How are you doing, Gerald?" Zach asked softly.

"I'm all right," Gerald replied unconvincingly. "But I'd be better if Hedy were here."

"You feel for her," Brad said.

"I ... I love her," he said. "I just wish she loved me back."

"She cares for you," Brad said. "Deeper feelings take time."

"I'm always in a hurry." Gerald shook his head. "That's what she keeps telling me: I need to take my time and not rush things."

"She's got some issues to work out," Brad said, torn between reassuring Gerald and telling him to run for his life while there was still time. *If* there was still time.

"I do everything she asks me to," Gerald said plaintively. "She didn't like what I was doing at FEMA, so I quit—just like that. She asked me to protect her and I'm doing that. So why doesn't she love me?"

"I'm sorry," Brad said. "I don't have an answer for that. But you probably need to think about another job now that you've left FEMA. What will you do?"

Gerald shrugged. "I don't know," he said. "I'm just waiting to see if Hedy asks me to stick around. Because if she doesn't then I have no reason to stay in New Orleans."

"You're not a native?" Brad suggested.

"I'm from Boston. I came here on a three-month contract to help rebuild the city. I never expected to fall in love..."

"How did you meet Hedy?" Zach asked.

"At a bar. I was doing card tricks for some of my buddies and she was at the next table. She seemed fascinated by the tricks, so I kept doing them even though I wasn't very good at it. We just sort of fell for each other. Well, I did. I think she just needed someone to unburden her sorrows to. Her husband doesn't treat her very well."

He stumbled and almost fell over.

Brad grabbed him by the arm. "Careful," he warned.

Gerald looked around the empty courtyard then turned his gaze to Hedy's door. "I better go. Tell her I came by, would you? Tell her I was checking up on her." He shook his head. "I'd die for that girl. I don't want anything to happen to her."

"Can we call a cab for you?" Brad asked.

"No. I'll be all right."

"Well, good night then," Brad said.

10

Morning brought a deceptive calm to the Marigny. A hush seemed to hold in the air. Even the usual banter of the birds was stilled. It might have been the stillness that preceded a storm, though the forecast had been for fair weather and blue skies as far as the eye could see.

Brad and Zach rose a little before eight and went to sit beside the pool. Derek brought out a tray of coffee and biscuits at 8:15. He set it on the table and glanced around.

"You've got the patio to yourselves, gentlemen," he said. "Enjoy it while you can."

At 8:30, Zach went for a swim. Brad read a morning paper, keeping his eyes peeled for items of interest in connection with the rebuilding of New Orleans.

It was just 8:45 when Quint arrived with his pail and mop.

"Hello, Quint," Zach called out, as he emerged dripping from the pool.

"Hello, Mr. Zach. You have nice blue hair."

"Thank you, Quint."

At nine o'clock, Mr. Sakamoto and Mr.

Nobutsugo came through the courtyard, bowed solemnly to Brad and Zach, and left.

Nine-thirty rolled around. Philip appeared with a fresh tray of hushpuppies. Brad put down his newspaper and asked for another coffee.

"Happy to oblige," Philip said, heading off.

He returned a few minutes later bearing a tray of coffee and condiments.

"No sign of Hedy yet?" Bradford asked, thinking it odd that Gerald hadn't put in his usual morning appearance. Perhaps he was too hung-over.

"Ah think she had a late one," Philip said, winking. "It's that boy keeping her up all night. We heard him come back around three in the morning. No doubt they had a good make-up session. Nothing like a little argument to stimulate young love."

Brad's phone rang. It was Grace phoning to say she'd just received the FBI file on Hedy.

"I hate to sound alarmist, but how is she?" Grace asked.

"I haven't seen her yet this morning," Brad answered.

"That's not good."

"Why?"

"Because the file says she's a wanted woman. And I don't mean in a good way. Can you find her?"

Brad glanced across the pool at Hedy's cabin. "Let me get back to you on that one."

It was right at that moment when a disturbing noise cut through the courtyard, a moan undercut by a terrified wail. The sound grew louder. What happened next was pieced together later and verified by three witnesses: Brad, Zach and Philip. Quint seemed almost to explode out of cabin number four, stumbling backwards down the stairs.

"Take care!" he screamed.

When he got to his feet, they saw that his T-shirt was smeared in blood.

"Quint, what's happened? What have you done to yourself?" Philip demanded.

"Take care!" Quint pointed to the cabin door.

The others looked, but could see nothing.

"Maybe the attacker's come back!" Brad cried.

He tore into the cabin, nearly tripping over Quint's overturned bucket and mop. Zach and Philip were right behind him. The trio stared in disbelief at the bed where Hedy lay, face up, her eyes staring vacantly at the ceiling. The sheets were stained red. A knife lay by her side.

Hedy's left hand dangled over the edge of the bed. On the floor beneath, a card had fallen as though she'd been clutching it when she died. Brad picked it up, tucking it in his pocket.

He ran to the window. It was locked and bolted. No one had come in that way. He turned back to the doorway where Quint stood shaking.

"Take care, take care!" the boy whimpered softly, as though warning the dead girl of something it was now clearly too late to avoid.

They watched as he came over to the bed and tried to scoop Hedy up in his arms.

"Quint! Put her down," Philip commanded.

The boy let Hedy's body fall back onto the sheets.

Philip shook him by the shoulders. "What were you doing?"

"We need to bury Hedy," he said with quiet desperation.

Philip shook his head. "Quint, you may not touch this body." He glanced at the knife. "Did you do this?"

The boy began to shake again.

Brad put a hand on Philip's shoulder. "I don't think it was Quint," he said. "I think he found Hedy lying here like this and got covered in blood when he tried to pick her up."

"We need to bury Hedy," Quint said quietly. "Or devils will eat her soul."

"That's utter rubbish!" Philip barked. It was the first time Brad had seen him come close to losing his composure. "There are no devils. The police will have to come and investigate. You may not touch Hedy again. Do you understand?"

"Yes." Quint nodded. "But Philip—who will bury her?"

"We will let the police determine that. It's not for us to decide."

The police arrived and began taking statements. The chief investigating officer was one DC Beaulieu, a man with heavy-lidded, bloodshot eyes that made him look not unlike a certain southern hound. Brad watched him go through the room, giving orders to his men to check under the beds and in the closets.

Beaulieu threw suspicious glances at Quint every few moments. The boy was a sorry sight. His arms and T-shirt were stained in blood and he burbled in fear whenever anyone spoke to him.

"I don't think this is what it seems, officer," Brad said after the man's third glance at Quint. "He's simple, but he wouldn't hurt anything, let alone a grown woman."

"Is that a fact, suh?" Beaulieu growled, giving Brad a scornful look.

Brad nodded. "I believe she was already dead when the boy came into the room to clean it. I think he was trying to help her when he got smeared with her blood. I know you have to question him, but try not to be too harsh. He's got a fragile mind. He was nearly beaten to death last year by a gang of thugs and left on the doorstep of the inn. He may have suffered some sort of brain damage."

The officer continued writing Brad's statements down, nodding every few words.

"We'll do more than question him, suh," he said, finally. "We all are going to arrest him for murder."

"Then that would be unfortunate, because he has a phobia about leaving the property."

Beaulieu snorted. "A phobia? Ah got a phobia about punks who kill women."

Brad realized he was getting nowhere. He let the officer continue with his work.

"That knife come from the inn?" Beaulieu asked Philip, looking over his shoulder at the weapon lying beside the body.

121

Philip shook his head. "Ah don't seem to recognize it."

The officer stared at him with his bloodshot eyes. "Is that a 'no,' suh?"

Unlike some men in uniform to whom you would gladly submit because of the thrill it would give to be ordered around by someone virile and attractive, these cops were the local goons and galumphs who neither cared nor dared to look attractive or flash a little sex appeal. Submitting to them would have proved about as pleasurable as kissing a pig's bottom. For Quint's sake, Philip remained his usual congenial self, but it seemed to require much greater effort than normal.

Philip nodded. "Yes, officer. It's a definite 'no'. The knife did not come from the inn."

"Thank you, suh."

Standing off to one side, Brad pulled out his phone. Grace picked up immediately.

"Too late," he said. "She's dead."

He'd never known his boss not to be behind the eight ball before.

"Then my advice is to stay out of it," Grace told him. "Both of you. I don't want you involved. Got it?"

"Got it," Brad said, clapping his cell shut.

The chief coroner had arrived. A giant of a man, his shadow filled the cabin doorway.

"Ah want this one wrapped up quick," Beaulieu told him. "Ah already got muh hands full with the others."

"'Others'?" Brad repeated.

"That's right, suh. Two grown men found

strangled with Mardi Gras beads over in Bywater last night." Beaulieu looked over at Brad and Zach. "Ah wouldn't recommend a walk down by the river any time soon."

When it came his turn to be questioned, Quint claimed not to know his last name.

Beaulieu turned to Brad. "Is this kid a wise guy?"

Brad shook his head. "I don't think so. As I tried to explain, he was beaten up and left for dead on the inn's doorstep about five months ago."

"We suspect Quint may have amnesia," Philip said. "He's been with us for the past four months. He's a very hard worker and he's never caused a bit of trouble. No one knows where he came from. Once he said he thought his last name might be Acme."

Beaulieu gave him a scornful look. "Spell that for me, please, suh."

Philip did so.

Brad sighed. Grace's words were still ringing in his ear. *I don't want you involved,* she'd said. Then again, he'd never been able to do what he was told. "I will vouch for this boy," Brad told him. He held out a card. "Call this number. I may be able to help with your investigation."

The officer took the card and examined it carefully, as though looking for flaws. "What are you, suh? A lawyer?"

"Special Investigations Unit. Out of state," Brad said simply.

Beaulieu looked over at Quint, who stood as though in a trance.

"If he didn't kill her then who did?"

"The night before last a man broke into the victim's room. She was staying in another cabin at the time. The owners offered her a room inside the inn for safety, but she refused. When I questioned her about the attacker, she said he had one side of his head shaved. She told us she didn't recognize him, but the next morning her husband showed up here and they argued over it. The husband told her to give him what he wanted so he would leave her alone."

"And no report was made?" The officer gave Brad a reprehensible look.

Philip looked stricken. "She insisted we not call the police."

The cop nodded. "Break and enter with potential threat of violence and y'all don't even call the police." He shook his head in disgust. "Some people. And what about the husband? Y'all said he showed up—is he staying here now?"

Philip shook his head. "No. Ah understand they were separated recently. She called him after the break-in looking for consolation. Ah doubt he gave her any."

"And what is the husband's name?"

"Ah believe his name is Tyrone Pritchard," Philip said.

The cop stopped writing and looked up. "The politician?"

Philip nodded. "The same."

Beaulieu shook his head gravely. His attitude seemed to change suddenly. He pulled out a cell phone and held it to his ear. "Get me

Superintendent Bayard," he said, heading outside so they couldn't hear his conversation. He returned within a few minutes, looking even less pleased than before.

"Anyone else come to see her? Boyfriends? Gentlemen callers?"

"Yes," Philip said. "There is a young man named Gerald, a former FEMA worker. He isn't staying here, but he was over frequently."

"When did y'all last see him?"

Philip looked at Brad. "He may have been here last night, but ah can't confirm it. When the husband showed up yesterday morning, Gerald ordered him to leave. There was some ill will between them."

The cop sighed and looked around. "Ah want a list of your guests. All of them."

"There's only one couple staying here besides these two gentlemen." He indicated Brad and Zach. "The others are a young Japanese couple. They aren't here now. They're booked to stay for another two days, but with what's happened they may decide to go elsewhere. If they do, ah will tell them to contact you first."

The officer nodded. "Thank you, suh. Ah must say, that is very efficient of you. It almost makes me think y'all have done this before."

Philip's mouth opened in surprise, but he said nothing.

Beaulieu looked over his shoulder at his fellow officers and nodded to Quint. "Take that one away, boys."

The officers came up and handcuffed the boy,

whose eyes were wild with confusion and fear.

"But Philip!" he cried. "Ah don't want to leave the garden. You said you and Derek would protect me!"

Philip's face was a mask of chagrin. "Ah'm sorry, Quint. Y'all have to go with these gentlemen. They won't hurt you."

The boy reacted with a ferociousness that gave even the hardened officers a fright.

"No! Ah cain't!" the boy cried, struggling. "Take care!"

It took four men to subdue him and remove him from the grounds, before placing him in the back of a cruiser where the medical examiner gave him a tranquilizer. Even Brad was astonished by the resistance he put up.

"Not exactly a meek little lamb now, is he?" Beaulieu said.

"I told you," Brad said. "He's frightened. He has a severe phobia about leaving the grounds."

"Whatever y'all call it," the cop said, "resistin' arrest is resistin' arrest."

He turned and went off to join his officers.

"What should we do?" Philip asked.

"Stay here and answer any further questions the police have," Brad said. "Let Derek know what happened when he returns. Zach will stay with you, in case you need any further advice. I'll go with Quint to the station. There's no telling what they might do to him if he resists any further."

"Take our car," Philip said, tossing him a key ring. "It's the Land Rover out back."

Brad caught the keys. As he turned toward the

gate, Philip clapped a powerful hand onto Brad's shoulders. "Look after him," he said. "Please make sure he's okay. He's a good boy."

11

Brad spent most of the evening sitting in an over-bright corridor in the Marigny police station. A cup of coffee and a newspaper were his only companions. As he'd expected, he wasn't allowed into the interrogation room for Quint's questioning. As a courtesy, following the questioning Officer Beaulieu came out to inform him of what he knew: nothing.

"Ah shouldn't be doing this," Beaulieu growled, "but if y'all have anything to help me out in this case, then y'all better let me have it."

"What have you got from him so far?" Brad asked.

The officer grunted. "Nothing. He claims he found the body in the cabin, like you said. Naturally, he would. On top of that, he ain't got no record."

"As I pointed out, Quint is a well mannered, simple-minded boy. At least he was, till you showed up and mistreated him. That boy is not a killer and that's why he's got no record."

The cop grunted again. "What ah meant was, there is no such person as Quint Acme nowhere in the country. That's why he ain't got no record, 'cause ah cain't find him."

Brad paused to let this fact sink in. A thought occurred to him. "Try Chester Morgenstern," he said. "You might find something there."

The cop shot him a doubtful glance. "Let's just hope ah do, because if not this kid is going to be in deeper and deeper shit the longer this takes." Beaulieu gave him a meaningful look. "Just so y'all know, ah am not giving up."

Bully for you, Brad thought. "Can I see him for a minute?"

"Ah suppose that won't hurt," Beaulieu said with a snarl. "But just for a minute."

Brad was led to Quint's cell. The boy looked up fearfully when the door was unlocked, but he calmed slightly when he saw Bradford.

"Please take me home," he pleaded.

Bradford shook his had. "I'm sorry, Quint. I am trying to get you out of here, but it's going to take some time. In the meantime, I will make sure you're safe and sound."

"At least the devils cain't get me here," he said with a pathetic sob.

"No, Quint. The devils won't get you. I promise you that."

"Thank you, Mr. Bradford."

It was just before midnight when Brad left the station, feeling helpless at being unable to provide any real comfort to the boy. Out in the streets, a wind was stirring in the tops of the trees. Clouds scudded across a blue-black sky. The night felt empty. Brad returned to the Lion's Roar to find

129

Zach, Derek and Philip gathered around the kitchen table in the main building. They looked up anxiously at his arrival.

"How's Quint?" Derek asked.

Brad told them he was unhurt, but that he had been unable to help him.

"At least he is all right. Ah was worried y'all might not get to see him," Philip said, shaking his head. "Ah can't believe that boy would hurt a puppy. Any fool could see that."

"Any fool but an official fool," Derek said.

"We'll have to convince them of that, if it comes down to it," Brad said. "You two have known him the longest, so you can vouch for him best."

"We will provide him with the best legal counsel available," Derek declared.

Brad walked around the table and kissed his boyfriend on top of the head.

"We've been busy while you were away," Zach said, nodding at the computer on the table before him.

"What's this?"

"Hedy's laptop."

Brad's mouth fell open.

"Ah grabbed it before the police arrived," Philip said. "Ah certainly hope ah did the right thing."

Brad gaped at him in amazement. "You sure did."

Philip smiled. "Knowing who Hedy's husband is, ah thought it made sense to ensure that any information on that thing is in good hands. Given the potentially sensitive nature of what it contains, of course. Once this little doll here"—he nodded at Zach—"has copied everything on the hard-drive, we can hand it over to the police. We'll just say she left it in the main building for safekeeping after the break-in and that we forgot about it in the excitement."

"Sounds like a plan," Brad said, impressed with their savvy.

"There wasn't much in Hedy's in-box," Zach said, "but I did a scan of her hard drive for erased messages and came up with something interesting. Take a look. The first note is to her boss, Willard Foster."

Brad bent to read.

Dear Willard,

I regret to inform you that I must hereby tender my resignation, effective immediately. You have betrayed my trust and the trust of the good people of Louisiana. You are a rogue and a scoundrel of the worst kind.

Hedy Pritchard

"There was no reply from Willard, but the same day Hedy received a note from her husband," Zach said.

Brad bent to read the second note.

Hedy,

Have you lost your cotton-picking mind? Willard tells me you quit your job and that you took an awful lot of his money when you left. What were you thinking, girl? He is going to have you charged with grand larceny if you don't return it. As your lawful husband, I order you to stop this nonsense. Need I remind you that this man is responsible for backing me in the political run-offs next year? Are you trying to blacken my reputation? In my estimation, that would be a very foolish thing to do.

Tyrone

Brad shook his head. "That's explosive stuff."

"It gets better," Zach said. "This is the reply Hedy sent the next day."

Brad scanned the final missive.

Dear Sir

It grieves me to have to tell you that I no longer consider myself to be your wife. As for the money—a significant amount of money which you and Willard stole together—do not think you can scare me into giving it back. If you force me to, I will destroy you

132

by any means that is in my power.
You know I can do that, Tyrone. I
have all the evidence I need to create
a scandal that won't go away for a
very long time.

Hedy

Brad looked at the faces staring at him around the table.

"So Hedy took money from her boss, claiming he and Tyrone stole it, and then threatened to expose them. That sounds like a strong motive for murder," Brad said. "I suppose either or both of them could have killed her."

"These southern girls are something else," Derek said, shaking his head. "I would hardly have believed Hedy capable of this."

"What about the means of entry into Hedy's cabin?" Brad asked Zach. "Did you find anything indicating how the killer got in?"

"No." Zach shook his head. "While Derek and Philip were talking to the police, I scouted the grounds beneath Hedy's window. It doesn't look like anything changed since the first break-in, which means her murderer walked right in the front door."

Brad shook his head. "After her scare the night before, it seems unlikely she would have left it unlatched."

Philip nodded. "Meaning it had to be someone Hedy let in."

"Like Gerald, you mean," Brad said.

"Ah suppose so."

"He's a possibility," Brad said. "So's her husband, though I doubt she would have willingly let him in after their argument."

"He would have to have rung at the front gate," Derek said. "Whoever came by last night didn't ring. Hedy must have been waiting at the gate when he arrived or we would have heard it."

Philip shrugged. "Unless she got drunk and called her husband again, which she might just have been crazy enough to do."

"Whoever it was could have phoned in advance," Brad said. "It also had to have been someone who knew she'd changed cabins."

"So we're back to Gerald," Derek said glumly.

"What about the letters? The ones in her drawer?" Brad asked.

Zach shook his head. "I didn't get a chance to look before the police made us leave the cabin."

Brad cocked his head. "We could look now. Of course, we'd have to break the police tape, but it wouldn't be fair to involve Philip and Derek."

Philip yawned. "Ah think it must be time for bed, don't you, Derek?"

Derek smiled. "I was just thinking that myself."

"Ah will lock this in mah office for safekeeping," Philip said, grabbing the laptop.

"Good idea," Brad said. "We'll figure out what to do with it tomorrow."

The two men headed off. Once they'd gone, Brad and Zach went out and scouted the courtyard. All was silent as they stepped over the yellow tape fencing off Hedy's cabin and unlocked the door.

Brad entered first, followed by Zach. The room was eerie in the moonlight. They closed the door behind them. Just then Hedy's cat gave a welcoming *meowr* that nearly sent both of them flying.

"Don't worry, kitty. Zach and I will make sure you find a good home," Brad said, feeling bad the cat had been neglected.

"I bet she could tell us what happened in here," Zach said. "If only she could talk."

Brad opened the drawer beside Hedy's desk and caught his breath. The letters wrapped carefully in pink ribbon that Hedy had shown him the previous evening were no longer there.

"Maybe the police took them during the search," Zach said.

"True, but what do you want to bet the letters won't show up on the list of evidence removed from the crime scene once a certain DA finds out what they contain?" Brad said.

"Thank goodness for Philip's resourcefulness in co-opting the laptop."

They went over the cabin from top to bottom, taking care to minimize the light seepage outside the window. Before leaving, they filled the cat's bowl with water and sprinkled some kibble onto a plate.

Tem minutes later, they were lying in bed facing one another.

"Let's not forget to forward copies of all the emails to Grace before we hand the computer over to the police."

"I'll make sure she gets them," Zach said.

135

"What I'm wondering is, can you restore the emails you found and make it look as though they were sitting in her in-box before we hand it over to the police?"

"Sure."

"Just to make sure they're easy to find."

"It's possible they will disappear too,' Zach said. "But at least that way we'll know who we can trust in the police force."

"'Trust' might be too strong a word," Brad said. "We might be able to cross a few names off our list of who to distrust automatically, at least."

Zach lay with his chin propped on one hand. Brad gave him an assessing look.

"This is great work you're doing. Grace is sure to be pleased."

"Thanks."

"How are you handling this? Murder is a hard thing to get used to."

"I'm okay," Zach said. "But it's still pretty hard to accept that someone killed Hedy for a pile of letters."

"For *evidence*," Brad reminded him. "They weren't just any letters. Who knows what crimes they alluded to specifically."

"I know."

"Hedy believed she was doing the right thing for the people of New Orleans—the poor and the dispossessed. I think she knew the risks. There aren't many people who would die to help others." Brad was watching Zach intently. "I would die for you. You know that, don't you?"

Zach took Brad's hand in his. "And me for you."

Brad turned to the bedside clock. It was nearly three AM.

"Let's get some sleep, Agent Kong. I have a feeling we'll both need to be fresh tomorrow."

12

Dc Beaulieu called just after six AM. Brad swore he could hear a rooster crowing somewhere in the background.

"Ah have news," the cop drawled in his distinctive Louisiana twang.

"Let's hear it," Brad said, trying to sound coherent.

"Your friend, Gerald McDormand, formerly of FEMA, made an unexpected visit to the home of one Tyrone Pritchard last night."

Brad groaned.

"Lucky for him he did not get to meet Mr. Pritchard in person. He did, however, manage to get himself arrested for break and enter and attempted assault."

Brad's mind leapt to the alert. "Assault? How so, if he didn't meet Pritchard?"

"He was unlucky enough to run into a statue in Mr. Pritchard's garden, which, in his inebriated state, he attacked with a hickory branch. Ah can assure you that in the state of Louisiana ah would have no trouble finding a jury to convict him of the above-mentioned charges, if Mr. Pritchard decides to press charges."

"For attacking a statue?" Brad cried in disbelief.

"Yes, suh!" There was the briefest of pauses. "On the other hand, the very same Mr. Pritchard has a vested interest in keeping his name clear of scandal and outta the papers at present."

"That's going to be difficult, considering his wife has just been murdered."

"On the contrary, ah have been led to believe that Mr. and Mrs. Pritchard have been separated for a considerable amount of time due to the emotional instability of Mrs. Pritchard and that the two were no longer in contact at the time of Mrs. Pritchard's ... unfortunate accident. And ah suggest you take an active part in making sure things stay that way."

Brad felt his gall rising. "In other words, you're asking for my silence in return for not pressing charges against Gerald. Silence for collusion, I believe they call it."

"Call it what you will," Beaulieu said. "All's fair in love and political shenanigans."

"So I've heard," Brad said.

"In any case, given the sensitive nature of this investigation certain things have yet to be classified as either problems or solutions, if you take my meaning..."

"Loud and clear," Brad said. "I'll stay out of it."

"And speaking of stayin' out of things, ah would certainly hope y'all wouldn't be stupid enough to withhold evidence from me."

Brad's ears pricked up. "Such as?"

"Y'all would know better than me, suh."

"I'll certainly be forthcoming if I hear of anything."

"In particular, a certain collection of personal correspondence between Mrs. Pritchard and her estranged husband might just top the list of items of interest, shall we say?"

"Are you talking about personal letters?" Brad asked in surprise.

"We might call it that, but ah have to remind y'all those are your words."

Brad was silent for a moment.

"Suh? Do y'all have anything to say on the matter?"

"Hedy did show us a pile of letters she said would be of particular interest to two political parties..."

"And?"

"They're not in her room now."

Beaulieu drew a deep breath.

Brad continued. "I looked in her desk drawer last night. They're gone. I don't know who took them."

"Ah see."

"It's the truth," Brad said. "Sounds like someone beat us both to them."

"That is most unfortunate for someone."

It certainly sounded like a threat, Brad thought. The only problem was, with Beaulieu's garbled speech it was impossible to say who was being threatened.

"Unfortunate for whom?" Brad asked.

"Ah would say that depends on who got to them

first and where they end up," Beaulieu said softly. "Most unfortunate."

"You seem to have overlooked one pertinent piece of evidence in all of this," Brad said.

"What is that, if ah may ask?"

"Hedy had a laptop."

The cop cleared his throat. "Ah believe we are already in possession of that particular item," the cop said. "Unfortunately, the hard drive has already been wiped clean."

"But—" Brad began.

"That is all ah have to say to you. Good day, suh."

The line went dead.

Brad turned to Zach, who was fully awake now.

"We better check the laptop."

They made their way to the main house, where Derek was just beginning his daily rounds.

"The office," Brad said to him. "We need to make sure the laptop is safe."

The door to the office was wide open. Hedy's laptop was gone.

"I can't believe it," Derek said, collapsing into a chair. "I feel responsible."

Two of the dogs sat watching the goings on.

"And what do you two have to say about this, Miss Muffet and Digger Dog?"

The pair looked away, as though ashamed of themselves.

Derek shook his head sadly. "Whoever broke in must have come armed with doggie treats, otherwise there would have been one holy ruckus last night."

"It's not your fault. You and Philip did your best." Brad turned to Zach. "Bad luck for us, though. Grace will crucify us for this."

Zach smiled. "Maybe not. I copied the letters while you were still at the police station. He held up a flash drive. "It's all on here."

"Thank goodness. Let's make sure Grace gets those right now."

Derek led Zach to another computer. In less than a minute, he installed the drive and sent the files off to Grace.

"Done," he said.

"That's a relief," Bradford told him. "If Beaulieu is to be believed, however, then there's another operative in this game of chess."

"How so?"

"They may have got the laptop, but Beaulieu claims not to know where the letters are. According to him, it's Pritchard who wants them. So if neither Pritchard nor the police have the letters, who does?"

"He could be lying to throw us off Pritchard's trail," Zach said. "Or maybe he doesn't know that someone else was working on his behalf. Clearly, whoever killed Hedy must have taken the letters. But why kill Hedy just to get the letters?"

"It may have been an accident," Brad said. "Maybe the killer didn't expect to run into her and she fought back."

"It was a pretty vicious killing," Zach said. "It seems clear that someone wanted her dead."

"If that's the case then she was killed to stop her from talking. Even if she gave up the letters, she could still tell what she knew. For all anyone knew, she might have had copies hidden somewhere. Killing her was the fastest way to prevent that."

"True," Zach said.

"Given the heated political debate in this state, my guess is that it could have been either side, one side wanting to expose the scandal and the other wanting to suppress it. Dirty political laundry can be very hard to clean. From what I know of Hedy, she wouldn't willingly have given those letters up to either side. They were her insurance to get what she wanted. Who's to say which side got to her first?"

Zach looked at him. "But the FBI filed warned against the attempt on her life. Is there any reason the FBI would want to save her life in this case?"

"Who can say? At any rate, the possibilities are pretty ripe for the picking. First off, there is an estranged husband with a big political future ahead of him. There is also Hedy's former boss, who is financing the husband's political career. Hedy seems to have stolen a considerable amount of money from them and threatened to expose them to charges of wrong-doing. These are very big stakes, no matter how you look at them. And then there's Gerald..."

"He doesn't seem to have had any motive for stealing the letters," Zach said.

"Not that we know of. But they might fetch a good price on the black market. What if Gerald needed money? It could be as simple as that. He quit his job at Hedy's say-so and then discovered she was about as flighty as a butterfly in a hurricane. Or who's to say he's not working for one of the parties? He might have pretended to be in love with Hedy so he could get his hands on the letters."

"But why kill her? She was out cold often enough that he could've just taken them if he'd wanted to. And she was drunk often enough that he could probably have convinced her to tell him if there were any copies."

"All true. Or maybe we just don't want it to be Gerald."

"What about the Japanese couple staying here?"

"I've thought of that," Brad said. "They don't seem the type, but that doesn't mean much. Anyone could have done it for gain."

"And you're still convinced it wasn't Quint?"

Brad shook his head. "That boy was too sensitive to hurt a fly. Also, if he did do it then why incriminate himself by picking her up and getting covered in her blood?"

"Because he might accidentally have got her blood on him while committing the murder, so he decided to go all the way."

Brad shrugged. "Yes, that's devious enough to make sense, but I don't see Quint as the devious type. He can barely speak proper English, let alone plan such a thing and expect to get away with it. No, I don't think it was Quint."

"Neither do I," said Zach. "My intuition says it wasn't him."

"Then again, how do we explain seeing him off

the premises twice?"

"Another mystery," Zach said. "Though we can't say for sure it was him we saw, so we shouldn't jump to conclusions."

"I keep going back to the night Hedy's room was broken into by the man with one side of his head shaved. We have no way of knowing who he is." Brad snapped his fingers. He dug into his pocket and brought out the card he'd found on the floor beneath Hedy's outstretched hand. "Of course, there's always this."

"What is it?"

"It's a clue. Hedy seems to have been clutching it before she was killed."

He held it up to the light. At first glance it appeared to be a standard business card, but in place of a business logo it had the glyph of a hand. The palm was divided into different regions designated variously as Mount of Luna, Plane of Mars, and Venus Girdle. The name on the card was "Doctor Doom, Seer and Prognosticator."

"Creepy," Brad said.

"Looks like Hedy was consulting a fortune teller," Zach said. "Maybe she wanted advice on her love life."

"A divorce counsellor might have been a better bet."

According to the card, Doctor Doom's office was located in Bywater within walking distance of the inn and not far from the warehouse where the Derelict Disco Spirit Raising party had been held.

Brad turned the card over. There, in looping figures, someone had scrawled *$500,000*. "No matter how good a fortune teller this Doctor Doom is, that's one hell of a consulting fee."

"You bet!" Zach exclaimed.

"I believe we have our day's work cut out for us, Agent Kong." Brad held out the card. "And this is where it starts."

13

Half an hour later the pair were on bicycles, heading in the direction of the abandoned warehouses huddled along the riverbanks. It took less than ten minutes to reach the address on the card, a small shack slightly apart from the other buildings. It hugged the riverbank next to the train tracks where a collection of boxcars idled in the morning sun. Closer inspection revealed they'd been there for some time, however. The wheels had rusted and the cars were stained by the same water lines that marked the sides of every building in town. Almost all were the same uniform shade of red-brown—all except one, that is. The exception was a peculiar off-white, with rusted flecks showing through. It looked as if all the colour had been leached out of it before being left to sit and rust.

A giant hand of fortune had been painted on the side of the warehouse. Underneath, it proclaimed: "Doctor Doom—Seek The Truth Here." The only problem was, the building sat behind a barbed-wire fence. Brad turned to Zach and shrugged.

"Are we not men, Agent Kong?"

"Sure we are, except when we're disco boys. I vote for the high-jump approach."

"I was thinking of something a little easier on the shins," Brad said, pointing to a hole in the fence roughly the right size for schoolboys to squeeze through.

"After you, Agent Red," Zach replied, holding open the compromised portion of the chain-link.

Brad slipped into the compound, keeping an eye out for signs of a security guard. So far, the grounds appeared deserted. Once inside the perimeter, they headed directly for the building. Close up they saw that its red brick façade was crumbling in places. As well, the enlarged hand was somewhat at variance with the usual palmists' associations of meanings attributed to the various lines and planes. The fate line was there, as were the lines normally associated with love and career, but the artist had departed from tradition by labelling the thumb and fingers as "Cadillac," "Disneyland," "Amazon," "Monopoly," and "Microsoft World."

They had just turned a corner and headed for the back of the building when a ferocious barking rent the air. Zach froze. Brad leaned down to grab a stick and held it up ready to strike.

Seemingly from out of nowhere, a monster Doberman leapt at Brad's throat.

"Look out!" Zach yelled.

Time seemed to contract as seemingly random memories flashed before Brad's inner eye. In particular, he recalled a party he'd attended as a teenager with half a dozen neighbourhood boys. Some had brought beer, others tequila—heady scores for under-aged kids. Another boy, a would-be hippie named Harris, had procured a particularly virulent form of black hashish mixed with opium, though neither Brad nor his friends knew it at the time. They had gathered in Harris's basement while his family were out bowling. After a couple of drinks, Harris brought out a hookah. None of the others had tried drugs before, but were eager to prove themselves. After just a few tokes of the potent concoction, Brad began to hear a phone ringing upstairs. When he mentioned it, Harris stared at him blankly.

"Dude—there's no phone ringing. You're just stoned."

The other boys sniggered and nodded. Brad listened. There it was again. No matter how the others denied it, the ringing persisted. At length, convinced it was his father calling to check on him, Brad went upstairs and picked up the receiver. To his amazement, all he heard was a dial tone. The ringing had been an aural hallucination brought on by the combination of drugs and alcohol and his own guilty conscience.

On his way home later that evening young Brad followed his usual path, creeping through the neighbour's darkened backyards. One house had recently acquired new owners, however, and Bradford hadn't traipsed across the property since they moved in. As he stumbled in the dark, he heard the clinking of a chain. Some atavistic

149

survival instinct clicked in as he realized it was a dog moving on its tether. He swerved mid-stride and tore off in the opposite direction just as a set of teeth nipped at his calf. Brad leapt out of range in the nick of time, quite sure that what he had heard was no hallucination.

Now, here in New Orleans, a somewhat older Brad was equally sure the dog he was seeing and hearing was real, not hallucinated, as it flew toward him through the air like a Ringwraith. Brad swung with his stick. Miraculously, it hit its mark. The animal yelped and fell to the ground.

Zach, meanwhile, had found a metal pipe. Gripping it firmly, he inched closer to Brad, closing ranks with his partner. The Doberman got to its feet and took stock of the situation, eyeing first Brad with his stick then Zach with his pipe. The creature looked wary but, like DC Beaulieu, it wasn't about to give up and run away.

Before anything could happen, however, the dog began to shiver all over. Mystified, Brad and Zach watched as it crumpled and fell to the ground then lay there without moving.

"That's weird. I barely even hit it," Brad exclaimed.

"That's good, because I doubt a stick would have stopped it. That was a monster of a dog."

Brad knelt and placed a hand on the Doberman's side. "It's dead," he said, with a bewildered expression.

"Odd it would die so quickly," Zach said. "It may have had a heart-attack."

"What's odder still is that it feels cool already,"

Brad said.

"Maybe the thickness of the fur keeps you from feeling the body heat," Zach suggested, placing his hand beside Brad's.

He, too, looked perplexed as he felt for a warm spot.

Brad reached for the collar and flipped the tag upwards till it glinted in the sun. The dog's name was "Gumbo." As he moved his hand, he disturbed the fur on the dog's neck, revealing a tattoo-like brand: "IV".

"Strange," he muttered. "I saw something like that on Quint's neck."

Brad looked across the yard. A row of sticks stood upright beside a series of mounds. He walked over to the first mound. In magic marker, someone had scrawled on the stick: *Gumbo I— September 2005*. Beside it was *Gumbo II*, who seemed to have lasted from October to November 2005, while *Gumbo III* was listed as having been born in December 2005 and buried in February 2006. They seemed to be in the middle of a dog cemetery.

"Seems like someone was very fond of the name 'Gumbo,'" Brad said. "And very fond of dogs, too. I hope we don't get charged with perricide."

"I just hope there aren't any more Gumbos around," Zach said, casting a furtive glance around the lot.

Just then a large man in a guard's uniform came running from one end of the building, shouting as he approached.

"Y'all stay right where you are," he

commanded, removing a Taser from his belt.

He approached wearing a suspicious look. Then he saw the dog lying on its side.

"What'd you do to Gumbo?" he demanded.

"We're sorry. He just ... died," Brad said with a shrug.

"Well, you're lucky," the man told them. "Gumbo would have torn you apart." He actually looked more relieved than angry. "This ain't the first dog to die like this," he said. "They all seem to have a short lifespan lately. I don't know what's wrong with them. I hope it's not some weird virus." He put his Taser away. "This is private property," he said, returning to the subject at hand. "What are you doing here, anyway?"

Brad held out the card. "We've come to see the doctor."

The man looked at the card and laughed. "The doctor," he said. "Well, then let's git you set up with him right away." He chuckled again, though Brad couldn't see the joke.

The guard pointed to a small doorway halfway down the building. "You go in that door and ask the little man inside to make you an appointment to see the doctor." He smiled and tried not to laugh again. "Good luck," he said. "Y'all give my regards to the doctor when you see him."

14

Brad approached the door with a primly-lettered "Caretaker" sign set in the centre. He knocked and entered. Zach followed. Inside, the air was cool. A wizened little man in a blue sweater with a plaid bowtie looked up over the brim of his glasses. It was Mr. Dress-Up crossed with Pee Wee Herman. His nose wrinkled as if the newcomers had let in a slightly distasteful smell.

"How m-m-may I be of assistance t-today?" he stammered, like some over-eager insurance salesman.

"We're here to see the doctor," Brad replied.

The little man's expression picked up. "That c-c-can be arranged, of course."

He made a show of looking over a large appointment book then looked back up at them. "W-w-when w-w-would you prefer?

"What's the next available appointment?"

The man shrugged. "I can probably squeeze you in the s-s-second week of June 2015." His expression suddenly turned mirthful. "Just a little j-j-joke. We're not too busy today. You can go in right n-n-now, if you like."

Brad shot Zach a glance. "Can he see us both at the same time?"

"Of course. What are your n-n-names?"

"Red and Kong."

"Uh-huh. Okay," said the man, biting his lower lip as he entered their names in a large ledger in careful script. "Mr. Red and Mr. Kong."

He looked up, eyeing them with suspicion. "You'll need quarters, of c-c-course. Do you have quarters?"

Brad felt in his pocket and shook his head. He turned to Zach who shrugged.

"Would you like me to make change for you?" The little man's smile brightened. "I like t–t-to make change!"

Brad took out his wallet and removed a five-dollar bill. "Will this do?"

"Perfect," said the little man, reaching into a drawer and expertly counting out the quarters one at a time so that they spun briefly before landing on the desk top. He'd obviously been doing this for some time.

Brad picked up the quarters, slipped them into his pocket and waited for further instructions.

The little man tugged on the ends of his bowtie. He pushed his chair abruptly back from the desk and beamed at them. "R-right this way, gentlemen."

They followed him through a fire door into the next room. Here the chill deepened and their breath came out in wisps. A curtain had been drawn across the far end of the room. Above it a sign proclaimed, "Doctor Doom—The All-Knowing

And All-Terrifying." Their host walked over to a wall and pressed a large red buzzer. Immediately, the sign lit up and the curtain pulled back to reveal a small machine the size of a jukebox. It stood before them, flashing and blinking. Brad thought it looked pleased to see them.

The little man looked at them expectantly. "Go ahead," he encouraged. "Put in a quarter."

Brad did as he was instructed. A voice boomed out, "What do you seek?"

The little man nudged him. "Go ahead. Ask a question."

"Uh..." Brad began. "What's four plus two?"

The machine burbled and finally spewed out, "The day is long and the grave is narrow."

"Try again," the little man urged. "Only this time ask a p-p-personal question."

"I, uh..." Brad shrugged. "I'm not sure what to ask."

"It's okay. I'll leave you in peace. I d-d-don't need to know what you ask, but you'll be amazed by the answers. Doctor Doom knows everything."

He left the room, quietly closing the door behind him.

Brad looked at Zach and shrugged. "Want to give it a go?" he asked, inserting another quarter.

Zach looked at the machine. It seemed to be waiting. "Who killed Hedy Pritchard?" he asked.

The machine began to huff and wheeze then made beeping noises. "Forget her. There will be others," it pronounced like a malevolent fortune cookie.

Brad put in another quarter. "How can we find

Hedy's killer?" he asked.

Again, the machine started to wheeze and gasp before finally spewing out its answer: "Intelligence is like shoe size. If the shoe fits, wear it."

Brad turned to Zach. "Should we read into that?"

Zach looked at him sceptically. "Somehow I don't think it's a Zen thing."

Brad turned back to the machine. "One more chance," he muttered under his breath, slipping a final quarter into its guts.

"What is going on in New Orleans?' he asked.

The machine grunted and belched its answer: "Beware! Darkness is falling."

Zach looked up to the sign "All-Knowing and All-Terrifying." He shook his head. "Do you think that's a metaphoric darkness or the literal kind?"

"We know it can't be a literal darkness," Brad said, looking at his watch. "It's just before ten o'clock in the morning."

At that moment, they heard a thunderclap. A cloud passed over the sun and all went dark outside the windows.

"Hmmm. Then again..."

Brad walked over to the door and knocked. It was opened by the tiny man.

"Finished already?" their host enquired with a hint of disappointment. Perhaps he feared they had offended Doctor Doom.

"That's all for now," Brad said.

The diminutive figure re-entered and pushed the red buzzer. The curtains slowly folded inward and the machine was laid to rest again.

"I h-h-hope you enjoyed your session," he said. "Did Doctor Doom reveal everything you n-n-needed to know?"

"Not quite. I have a few questions for you, if you don't mind."

"Not at all," the caretaker agreed eagerly. "If you're wondering about s-s-setting up a franchise, it can be easily arranged. Doctor Doom is quite p-p-profitable. Many seek his advice." A look of chagrin crossed his face. "When we haven't recently been d-d-devastated by a natural disaster, of course. But they'll be back. You can m-m-mark my words. Plus, we also do karaoke Fridays. Doctor Doom chooses s-s-songs to match your mood!"

"It's actually more a matter of police business," Brad said, hoping he wouldn't ask for identification.

The man was instantly cowed by the phrase "police business."

"I have a license," he said, pointing to a framed document on the wall behind him.

"It's not that," Brad said.

"Of course, I'll do anything I c-c-can to help," he said, nervously straightening his bowtie.

"I just wondered if a young woman named Hedy Pritchard has been to visit Doctor Doom in the last couple of days. She would be about five-two, slim build, attractive, with dark hair and a sad expression."

The little man reflected for a moment. "Yes, I believe someone of that general description c-c-came by last week. I c-c-couldn't say for sure without seeing a photograph."

"Has the doctor seen many people this week? Apart from us, I mean."

The little man looked off and appeared to reflect on this. "No," he stated. "I wouldn't say 'many'."

"How many would you say, if you were to hazard a guess?"

"Well, that's ..." He sighed and his shoulders slumped. "Just one. We haven't been busy since K-Katrina. But I'm sure things will pick up. Doctor Doom is an authority in his f-f-field and people surely will recognize his importance."

"Were you present when the young woman asked her questions of Doctor Doom?" Brad asked. "I know it's breaching confidence, but it could be important. If you know anything, please tell me."

"Dear me," said the tiny figure. "I'm n-n-not sure what to tell you. I could see she had a lot of concerns on her mind. Heartache was etched all over her f-f-face. As for her actual questions, I did not listen in. I generally d-d-don't. It's only when the customer is comfortable with my p-presence that I actually stay in the room. Far too many people come for c-c-confidential answers to some very private concerns. It's not m-m-my business to pry. Oh, no!"

His expression seemed to suggest he was aghast at the notion that he might eavesdrop on his clientele.

Brad shivered. His breath came out in little wisps when he spoke.

"Why do you keep it so cold in there?" he asked.

"Oh!" the little man exclaimed. "Doctor Doom prefers it that way. M-m-my goodness, but you certainly are the curious type."

"You're not the first person to suggest that," Brad said with a smile. "Thank you for your time, sir. We are much obliged to you."

"Oh, don't thank me," the little man said effusively. "Thank Doctor Doom!"

Once they were out of earshot, Brad turned to Zach. "Am I entirely off centre or was that just about the strangest thing you've ever seen?"

"Close," Zach concurred. "I once saw a Buddhist monk transmigrate into the body of a cobra to terrify some developers who were threatening to tear down a monastery."

Brad blinked.

"But other than that, I think you're right," Zach said. "What's a strange old man doing babysitting a fortune-telling machine in the middle of a wasteland where no one goes? Is it a Louisiana thing or is it just a wry, post-modern comment on contemporary life?"

"I side with the latter," Brad said. "But let's just say where *almost* no one goes. I'd give a lot to know what Hedy came here for."

"I'm with you there."

"And the cold!" Brad shivered. "Why so chilly?"

"That's not so hard to understand," Zach said. "It's a controlled environment. As he said, Doctor Doom prefers it that way. In this humidity and with the constant heat, machines probably tend to break down quickly."

"Brrr!" said Bradford. "No franchises for me. I won't share my lodgings with a snowman, that's for sure. Did he win?"

"Win? Who?"

"The monk. Did he manage to scare the developers off?"

"Not the first time. He had to come back a second time as a Bengal tiger before he could get them to back off. He eventually turned things around, though."

Brad regarded his partner. "It's always colourful with you around."

Zach smiled. "That's my job."

They looked back at the railway line running behind the building. The odd-coloured car seemed to stand out even more in the morning sun. From a distance, they could just make out the words DANGER—REFRIGERANT. The flecked paint made the metal look fuzzy, as though it had been coated in glue and dipped in lint. A closer inspection showed a light frosting on the outside.

"Now that's cold!" Brad exclaimed.

"I wonder if there's a connection between the tank and the sub-zero temperatures Doctor Doom requires for his Wizard of Oz hat trick," Zach said.

Brad smiled. "Good question. Let's ask the doctor next time we see him."

They trudged back across a desolate, sun-baked field littered with broken bricks. A lonely weed sprang up here and there. In the distance a sign read GARDEN. Brad looked around at the desolation. It seemed yet another of New Orleans's post-modern comments on contemporary urban living in the aftermath of almost total annihilation.

Once again, Zach held open the fence to allow Brad to slip through. On the far side, they turned back to look at the office sitting in the morning sun. From a distance, the hand of Doctor Doom appeared to be waving an ironic goodbye. Though it lay within the city limits in a fairly populated area, the building seemed oddly isolated. Brad wondered what it had originally been built for.

"My guess is it was once a slaughterhouse," he said.

"Another question for Doctor Doom," Zach replied.

"I suspect all the good doctor would be able to tell us is something like, 'A stitch in time saves nine' or 'All things come to those who wait.'"

"Or 'Every good boy deserves fudge'," Zach suggested.

"That too. In any case, we can't afford to forget that Hedy seems to have visited this place with some purpose in mind. I think we should come back here tonight after dark. Or should I say, 'When darkness falls'?"

"Hmmm," Zach said. "Is that a metaphoric or a literal darkness?"

"That," Bradford replied, "remains to be seen."

Back at the Lion's Roar, a call to Grace ensued. Brad tried to describe the situation down at the waterfront and their encounter with the all-knowing, all-terrifying Doctor Doom.

"Quarter a throw? Not bad, I guess. I used to

161

get worse advice from some of the directors here," Grace told him. "And by the way, that was excellent work from Agent Kong retrieving those emails. Make sure you tell him. Unfortunately, there's no way to prove where they came from without the laptop, especially if it comes down to a murder trial in Louisiana where bought juries are a dime a dozen."

"What else should we do then?"

"Carry on. What else can you do?"

The line went dead.

15

Night-time found Brad and Zach on the streets of Bywater once again. They passed a vacant lot where someone had arranged a sofa and chairs in the semblance of a living room out under the open stars. Something glowed softly at the centre, a light emanating from an ancient black-and-white television broadcasting from the middle of the otherwise empty lot. The blurred images flickered as though they'd been dredged up from the far end of some peculiar universe.

From somewhere close by came a howling that sent shivers up Bradford's spine. Other voices chimed in with excited little yips and yelps, like a wolf pack set loose within the city limits.

"I hope we're not about to run into Gumbos V, VI and VII," Brad said. "Whatever that is, it sounds awfully frenzied."

"It's a pack howl," Zach said. "They're hunting something down."

"At least we're prepared this time," Brad said, brandishing the Taser he'd bought at a local Walmart.

The howling grew closer then suddenly veered

away from them. The silhouettes of the deserted warehouses loomed. Shadowy figures moved in the distance. It seemed as though the action was happening down by the river. Brad suddenly recalled Beaulieu's warning that whatever was going on in the Bywater District late at night might not be particularly beneficial to one's health.

"Stay close to me," he warned Zach.

They continued on till they reached the office of Doctor Doom. The "Caretaker" sign hung slightly askew. All was dark inside.

"It seems the good doctor is not in this evening," Brad said quietly. "That's welcome news for us."

They crept up to the building, keeping a sharp eye out for any of Gumbo's relatives. Peering through a window into the reception area revealed nothing. There wasn't so much as a Coke machine or even a nightlight to brighten a silhouette or mark an outline for would-be intruders intent on entering the premises—intruders like the pair lifting the window and hoisting themselves over the sill at that very moment.

Once inside, they quickly examined the waiting room with their penlights, but found nothing apart from a handful of Sudoku books and a pile of business cards stacked on the caretaker's desk. Not surprisingly, the appointment book turned out to be full of empty pages, one date after another dutifully outlined in pencil. It was just as the caretaker had said. Only when they came across the date Hedy visited was there any indication that something had occurred on that day. In a timid scrawl, heavily underlined, was the figure $500,000—precisely the amount pencilled on the back of the card she had dropped at her deathbed.

Brad pointed this out to Zach, who nodded solemnly.

"I'd call that a 'significant amount of money,'" he said, quoting Hedy's accusatory email to her husband.

Having finished with the lobby, they moved on to the cold room where Doctor Doom was housed. The curtain was drawn closed and the room lay in shadows, much as it was when they visited earlier in the day. Brad slipped behind the curtain and found himself in utter darkness. He reached for his penlight, but it slipped from his hand and clattered to the floor.

"Damn," he muttered.

As he groped around in the darkness, he accidentally bumped into Doctor Doom. Suddenly the curtains parted and the machine whirred to life, flashing and blinking.

"The one you seek is alive!" proclaimed Doctor Doom, as Brad scrambled to his feet. "Beware when you meet him again!"

Bradford made a furious stab at the buttons on the console in an effort to silence it.

"You always hurt the one you love," Doctor Doom prophesied, spewing forth malevolence and gloom at the presumed seekers of truth who had come to reap its unparalleled wisdom.

Zach rushed to Brad's aid.

"How do you get this thing to stop?" Brad hissed.

"Love will only break your heart," continued the machine, its advice unasked.

Zach slipped behind Doctor Doom and disappeared in the dark.

"Beware! The darkness is f-a-a-a-a-a-l-g-r-h," The machine suddenly flat-lined and the curtain closed over Doctor Doom's mysterious figure as Zach emerged with the end of a cord in his hand.

"Oh—right," Brad said. "I should have thought of that."

Finding nothing more, they slipped back out through the window. The howling had stopped. Silence reigned as they headed for the abandoned warehouses.

"Let's split up and take a quick look around the perimeter," Brad suggested. "I'll go left and you go right. We'll meet up on the other side."

"Sounds good to me," Zach said. "See you in a few minutes."

Brad waited till Zach melted into the shadows then headed to the far side of the building where nothing but the stars brought a glimmer to the grounds. He was just about to turn the corner when he glimpsed someone slipping stealthily across the fields, as insubstantial as a cloud whirling past in the night sky. Brad held his breath and withdrew into the shadows as the figure passed within three feet of him, never for a moment sensing his presence.

Whoever it was seemed to know his way around. There was no hesitation, even in the pitch dark. Brad followed at a distance as his quarry headed for a far corner where odds and ends of junk were piled everywhere. The figure wandered slowly around as though looking for something. He hadn't far to look. There, not ten yards ahead, Brad could make out the silhouette of two men kissing. They were in a gay cruising ground.

The newcomer stopped to regard the pair, then silently stepped up to the lovers, reaching out to grope first one and then the other. Neither seemed to mind. In fact, they seemed inclined to include him in their amorous play, trading inquisitive kisses with him.

It wasn't long before the kissing turned into heavy petting. T-shirts were stripped off and tossed overhead. The original pair now had the newcomer between them. The taller one slid his hands under the man's belt and undid the clasp, letting his shorts fall to the ground. Brad felt a tinge of lust as the man in the rear spit onto his palm, greased his formidable erection and quickly entered the newcomer, who groaned in pleasure.

From slow and gentle, the thrusting grew in force till the middleman was literally lifted off the ground each time his partner shoved into him. The action took on a rhythm. Brad knew he'd overstayed his welcome, but he hung back a moment longer. A groan warned of imminent orgasm as the man in the middle was lifted even higher.

Seemingly from nowhere, they were surrounded by a half-dozen men yipping and yelping. As the man in the middle shouted out in orgasmic frenzy, the man riding him suddenly gripped his head, wrenching it sideways with a loud snap. Brad watched the third man catch the limp body and let it slump to the ground. As he did so, the group howled as one.

Brad was horrified, but even with his Taser he wasn't about to confront the gang, now numbering a dozen or more. He needed to find Zach and warn him. Shaken, he slipped off into the shadows as he suddenly remembered Doctor Doom's prophecy.

"What is happening in New Orleans?" Brad had asked.

"Beware! Darkness is falling," came the answer.

"Doctor Doom knows everything," claimed the peculiar little man in the waiting room.

Yes, Doctor Doom was highly impressive, indeed.

Brad reached the far side of the warehouse and looked around—no Zach. His heart began to pound. Had Zach run into those deadly punks in the dark? He prayed not. Just then, he heard light footsteps and turned to see a familiar figure coming toward him.

"Thank God you're here!" he whispered, but that was as far as he got.

16

Brad woke from a dark and troubled sleep. Opening his eyes, he found himself in a sombre landscape marked by long, empty avenues. Miniature houses lined the streets, each slightly larger than the height and breadth of a human being. He wandered alone through this twilight place, hearing nothing but his own breathing. The silence was more startling than any sound. At one point a crow cawed raucously overhead, but when he looked up no bird was visible to the eye. Dead leaves clung to the trees as if no wind had ever stirred the branches in this place. Shadows moved silently about though, strangely, they seemed not to be attached to anything.

A pressure inside his head prevented Dan from focusing his vision. Everything looked hazy. The air felt heavy, like an invisible fog, as though the darkness had been compressed and condensed. Glancing up at the street signs, Dan saw the avenues were laid out in a series of interconnecting rows, but following them proved a challenge. Avenue A might suddenly join up with Avenue Q or Z, which in turn led to Avenue P and so on. Everything was completely unpredictable and strangely unreal.

The tiny houses were locked and silent within. Odder still, none of them had windows, although some had openings below the roofline for the air to pass through, if there were ever a breeze to move it along. Bradford began to make out dates and names inscribed on the outer walls of these miniature houses. One name stood out among all the rest: *Marie Laveau*. For some reason it rang a bell, but he couldn't think why.

Brad's feet were almost too tired to lift. His footsteps echoed hollowly between the houses. A thought struck him: everything in this strange town was made of stone. The trees with their withered leaves and even the animated shadows seemed to be made of solid rock. And he, Bradford, was slowly petrifying too.

He suddenly found himself surrounded by a horde of ghouls. Their flesh hung in strips; their eyes were crazed and bloodshot. When he tried to run, Brad found he could move only in slow motion. With a Herculean effort he reached a gate. Looking over his shoulder, he saw the ghouls in even slower pursuit. Determined to get back to the outside world Dan shook the gate, but it was padlocked. Grabbing the iron grille, he hoisted himself up. He had just got his right leg over the top when one of the ghouls caught his left foot. Shaking it as hard as he could, he sent the creature flying.

The sudden release catapulted him over the wall. He landed with a thud on the other side.

170

Normal movement suddenly resumed. Colour returned to his vision as the world came alive again. When he turned to look back the ghouls were snarling and frothing, reaching arms through the bars to grab him. A sign hung overhead: *City of the Dead*.

Brad blinked. The morning light was harsh. His head echoed with the sound of a thousand buzz saws. When he reached up, his hand came away smeared with blood from a gash on his temple. Shielding his gaze from the sun, he sat up. From the looks of it, he was lying outside a deserted warehouse. Somehow it looked familiar. Yes, it was coming back to him now ... he'd been creeping around the night before when suddenly everything had gone black and ... *Zach!*

He'd just found Zach right before the lights went out.

Brad struggled to his feet and looked around. Zach was nowhere to be seen. He knew Zach would never have left him lying there. Something must have happened to him. Something terrible. And he, Bradford Fairfax, was responsible. With a sinking feeling, he remembered the shadowy figures and the ritualised killing he'd witnessed in the cruising ground. Unlike the decrepit ghouls of his nightmare, they had all been physically perfect specimens.

He looked down at his wrist and saw that his watch was missing. He reached into his pocket. Both his cell phone and wallet were gone as well. Whoever had taken his phone would be stupefied to find that every number required a special code.

Taking it apart meant setting off a very loud alarm. Both the watch and wallet contained a tracking device, but they weren't important now. What he was concerned about was his partner. Whoever knocked Brad out must also have done something to Zach.

His head felt woozy. Walking was hard going, the simple act of putting one foot in front of the other requiring an extreme act of concentration. He was reduced to taking baby steps till he got the hang of it again. Who said childhood was wasted on the young? They could keep it.

Looking around, he saw there was no one else about. For a moment he wondered if he was still dreaming. It was more colourful here than in the City of the Dead, but just as empty. Then he remembered: it was Sunday. You may have been out boozing and playing cards with the boys or stayed up all night carousing with the girls, but come Sunday in Louisiana, whether rich or poor, hung-over or stone-cold sober, you went to church even if you weren't spiritually inclined. Those were the rules.

Just then a bell gonged. The tone was so loud—or at least it seemed so to Brad—that it nearly knocked him off balance. The chime sounded repeatedly, making him cover his ears. When it finally died out, he looked up to see a sign: *Seek Ye The Truth Here*. Maybe this was one of Doctor Doom's franchises.

The legend TABERNACLE OF THE TRUE VINE had been etched in stone over the lintel. An event board next to the door read, "I am the true vine, and my Father is the gardener." The theme for today's sermon was, "Sin, Degradation and the Vermin in Christ's Garden", to be followed by a treatise on "The Five Visitations From Hell." It sounded like the ecclesiastical version of a slasher flic, Brad thought. In any case it was a church, so there would be people inside to help.

He stumbled through the door. Sunlight streamed in after him, outlining his figure like the arrival of a derelict messiah. The pastor was in the midst of a sermon, shaking his fists in evangelical fervour.

"Every man is vile and depraved!" he cried. "We are born into depravity and we live as miserable sinners on this pestilential cipher called earth."

And great joy be unto you too, Brad thought.

The place was empty except for two men with their heads bowed—probably in sleep, not prayer— as well as an old lady clutching a purse and dressed to the nines, and a young boy who watched Brad with huge, frightened saucers for eyes as though he were the devil incarnate.

The pastor looked up at Brad's entrance. "Welcome, sinner," he cried out. "Have you come to be saved?"

"Uh ... I guess I have," was Brad's response, thinking he'd better explain that he'd been attacked and robbed.

"We don't *guess* in God's house!" the preacher roared. "In God's house, we *know!* And what we *know* is that we are all born vile and depraved. Rejoice, sinner! *Amen!*"

173

At that point, the men Brad thought were asleep lifted their heads to mutter two of the feeblest *Amens!* he'd ever heard.

"Do you by any chance have a telephone?" Brad asked. "I was attacked. I need to call the police."

A frenzied light shone in the pastor's eyes. "The telephone is the devil's invention! Come up here and be saved, sinner! Repent! God's wrath is visited upon you. Tell us your sins and be redeemed. The hour is at hand."

Brad had heard these End-of-Days sermons before. He never understand the slow, patient waiting of the righteous, as though one day God would suddenly decide He'd had enough and take revenge on the wicked and ungrateful. Why hadn't He simply created better people? Why all this disappointment in something you'd made yourself when you could just chalk it up to poor craftsmanship and get on with a new improved model, like software systems and Blackberries? It seemed futile to expect superior results from inferior models.

"Uh, maybe another time. Thanks anyway," Brad said, turning to leave.

Out on the street, he flagged a cab. The driver slowed, took one look at his bloodied clothes then zoomed off as fast as he could. A second cab stopped, but he too sped off when Brad tried to explain that he had no money to pay for the ride. Eventually, he began to walk. Even the street people avoided him. They took one look at his ragged state and made for the far side of the road. Twelve very long blocks later, he arrived at a police station.

The officer on duty stared a hole in him. "Couldn't find anything better to do than pick a fight on a Saturday night, fellow?"

"I was attacked," Brad said. "My partner has gone missing and I may have witnessed a murder."

"A murder?" The man shot a hard look at him. "Are you saying you *know* you saw a murder or you maybe *think* you saw a murder?"

He was beginning to sound a lot like the manic preacher.

"I'm pretty sure. I'd like you to contact DC Beaulieu of Fifteenth Division."

"Beaulieu don't work daytimes or Sundays. This happens to be both."

He reached under a counter and brought out a form. With a sniff, he tossed it on the countertop where it came to rest under Brad's nose.

"Fill in your name and the date and write a brief description of what happened," the cop told him.

Brad glanced over the form then looked up. "I don't suppose you have a pen?"

The officer pursed his lips. "I'll give you mine if you promise not to goober on it."

Brad nodded. The man handed it over with a look of disgust. Brad's fingers trembled as he filled in the answers. When he passed back the completed form, the cop looked it over quickly and sighed.

"What exactly are you hoping we can do for you?"

"I want you to find my partner," Brad said. "He

175

might have been hurt or worse."

"I'll have someone look into this," he said, nodding at the form. "You go on home and get some rest."

Brad slammed both hands on the counter and leaned as far across as he could. "Someone needs to look into this right away!"

"Ain't nobody here right now to do any lookin'. As for a possible murder, this city is now officially the murder capital of the US. We already got plenty to look into. For now, I'll file the report."

"This is an urgent matter!" Brad said, struggling to restrain his anger. "It's life or death. You need to do more than file a report."

The cop shrugged. "All I can do is file the report, bub. You all wanta hope your friend is alive and well and maybe he just walked off under the influence somewhere. Likely he'll turn up tomorrow and all will be fine. In case you haven't noticed, we got bigger problems right now. This is a small fire for us all."

"If you'd like, I could start a bigger one."

The cop gave him an aggravated look. "I think you all better go home and sleep it off—"

"I'm not drunk!" Bradford roared. "I've been attacked and my partner is missing. Someone could have caused him serious harm. Isn't that where you come in?"

The officer stared him down. "Let me do the math for you. I got three calls for B&E, one for assault, two for armed robbery, and another for attempted homicide. Plus, it's a Sunday morning and I only been on duty fifteen minutes. Go on home now and I'll file the report. Otherwise, I might just lose it altogether."

If Brad could have, he would have dragged the cop over the counter and pummelled him into the ground. Knowing that he had better ways of dealing with the situation, he simply turned and left the station.

17

Bradford Fairfax was more devastated by his partner Zachary Tyler's disappearance than almost anything he'd endured in his relatively short life. He'd lost his mother when he was four years old and his father eleven years later, leaving him very much on his own. At that point he was made a ward of the courts. Later, a small inheritance stood him in good stead to help him enrol in university in a joint journalism and world politics degree, where he'd aced all his courses.

Without family he thought his life by rights would be a lonely one, but since meeting Zach something like joy slowly crept into his life. How cruel then to find the perfect partner only to have him snatched away again. One thing Brad knew for certain: he would do everything to get him back. "I would die for you," he'd told Zach earlier that week. If he had to, then now was the time to prove it.

He turned his gaze to the sun—Quint's "big yellow ball"—and felt a searing pain hit the back of his eyeballs. He stumbled as he walked. He knew he should go to a hospital and get checked for concussion, but he couldn't think about that right now. He needed to focus on finding Zach.

Leaving the police station, Brad headed back to the river. Over the next two hours he checked out every single warehouse in the district. All stood derelict and abandoned. None showed any signs of life, not even vagrants or homeless people, which was odd given the city's negative vacancy rate. Odd, that is, until you considered the murderous tribe roaming the waterfront after dark.

Exhaustion was kicking in. Brad knew he should rest. He had to be sharp to continue his search. Right now, he was too frazzled to go on. He stumbled back to the Lion's Roar in the intense afternoon heat. The police tape was still in place across the doorway to Hedy's room. He was grateful not to run into Derek and Philip and have to endure their solicitous attention.

Back in his cabin, he dug through his luggage till he found his spare cell phone then put in a call to Grace. She listened as he described the unauthorized search that he and Zach had made of the warehouse grounds and the band of roving punks with lethal tendencies.

"I hate to think Agent Kong got a rotten deal on his very first assignment," she said quietly, "though it would be no less grievous if it were his hundredth. I'm sorry, Red. I'll mobilize all our assets in your area. We'll do whatever we can. Forget the local cops. They're still as corrupt as ever, from the sounds of it."

Brad sighed.

"Agent Red?"

"Yes?"

"He's a big boy and he's been well-trained. I don't think I need to mention that he is also possessed of some highly astounding skills that not every agent has. Leave the worrying to me and do your best to try to find him. Let me know the moment you learn anything pertinent."

Click.

Pertinent, Brad thought scornfully. For fuck's sakes—what the hell does "pertinent" mean?

He glanced around the cabin. Normally, Zach was meticulously tidy, but he'd left a T-shirt spread out on the bed as though he'd intended to wear it later. It was blue with three schooners printed on the front in red, black and yellow. Brad had bought it for him not long after they'd met. He picked it up and smelled it, inhaling the fragrance deep into his lungs. Zach's scent was strong, that sweet man-boy smell of freshly-scrubbed skin. His toothbrush sat on the bathroom counter. Brad gripped the vanity to steady himself. He looked in the mirror and cursed what he saw—a man who had let his partner be taken from him.

His hair was matted with dried blood and sweat. Dust streaked his nose and cheeks. Grime was caked on his chin and down his neck. He managed a smile. No wonder even the street people had avoided him. He looked like an extra from a zombie film.

Brad slid onto a chair and fell asleep. It was late afternoon when he woke to the phone's ring. Sergeant Beaulieu was on the line. The cop had received his written report. He asked brusquely if there'd been any update on Zach's status.

"None, and I doubt there will be any until you get out there and look into whatever's going on in that area."

"Ah've got my men looking into it. They'll make a thorough search of the area." He paused. "Do y'all think this might have anything to do with the murder of that young woman at the Lion's Roar?"

"No," Brad said then caught himself. "Sort of."

He didn't need to be charged with obstructing a murder investigation on top of everything else.

"Ah hope y'all haven't been holding out on me again."

"No, nothing like that," Brad said, not sure he was ready to hand over the one slim bit of evidence he had—Doctor Doom's business card—to a corrupt police force. "It's just that Hedy mentioned having seen a fortune teller. We went looking to see if we could find one."

"Ah shouldn't have to tell you not to go investigatin' on your own...," Beaulieu began. "Anyway, the city's full of fortune tellers. It's part of the culture."

"This one operated in an old office down along the river in the Bywater district."

There was another brief pause. "Y'all aren't referring to Doctor Doom by any chance?"

Brad started at the mention. "You know Doctor Doom?"

Beaulieu snorted. "Sure. The wife and ah used to go down to Friday karaoke nights sometimes ... before the storm, anyway."

Figures, Brad thought. "I'm still not convinced

there's a connection. Hedy's murder seemed personal, but this attack was totally random. Wrong place at the wrong time."

"Well, y'all just hafta leave it to us," Beaulieu said.

That's the last thing I intend to do, Brad thought.

Beaulieu was about to hang up when Brad thought of Quint.

"Wait! How's Quint, er, Chester Morgenstern?"

"Fine enough for a murder suspect."

"Were you able to pull up anything on him under that name?"

Beaulieu grunted. "Mah boys are still workin' on it," he said without conviction. "Y'all hafta remember things don't move quite as fast down heah as they do up north. Ain't no good rushin' things."

With that attitude, Brad thought, it's a wonder the sun even bothers to rise over Louisiana. He listened as Beaulieu made a few not overly reassuring promises to do everything in his power to find Zach then hung up.

Bradford walked over to the main house and knocked. Philip let him in. Briefly, he outlined what had happened the previous night. They were greatly disturbed by the news. And, given his condition, they advised him to seek medical assistance.

"No time right now," he said. "I need to keep looking for Zach."

"We'll help," Derek said.

Brad shook his head. "I can't involve you in

this. Besides, you need to be here if the police come back to look the place over."

A look of concern crossed Derek's face.

"What is it?" Brad asked.

"I'm not sure it's anything, but Mr. Nobutsugo and Mr. Sakamoto haven't returned since Hedy's murder. Do you think it's a coincidence?"

Brad shrugged. "Hard to say, but be careful of having anything to do with them beyond your normal routine if they come back."

Unwilling to sit around and wait any longer, Brad struck out across the city. As he walked, a spell of dizziness overtook him. Enticing smells wafted by. It had been nearly twenty-four hours since he'd eaten.

His steps took him to Café du Monde, home of the *beignet*, a rectangular, deep-fried doughnut served warm and piled with heaps of icing sugar. Along with succotash and grits, it was considered a southern delicacy.

Brad sat at a table, fighting a wave of nausea. The young Asian woman who took his order was the very image of militaristic fervour. Dressed in a black halter top, pleated skirt and army boots, she rolled her eyes on seeing his bandaged forehead. Another drunken idiotic tourist, her expression read. She performed her job with frightening efficiency and seemed to resent any hemming and hawing on his part as he glanced at the menu. No loafers here, was her attitude.

After he'd ordered, Bradford looked around the open-air café. With little more than a roof to keep out the rain, the interior was subjected to gusts of wind and the occasional pigeon that thought it had landed on easy street with all the tourists' leftovers. Outside on a crosswalk, the usual collection of hawkers and buskers had taken up positions. A tuba player and violinist performed Pachelbel's never-ending canon, while on the opposite corner a man named Captain Crawdaddy—a cross between Screamin' Jay Hawkins and Howdy Doody—bellowed Cajun songs. Competition was fierce.

A few tables away, positioned carefully out of Brad's line of sight, sat a man with one side of his head shaved. Brad was too preoccupied to notice him as he pondered what had become of Zach and what he might do should anything dire have befallen him. He suspected he would be unable to face himself if it came to that.

His server returned bearing a plate of *beignets* and a café latte, thumping them onto the table with a show of disdain just to prove she wasn't his server by choice. Then she huffed off again.

The plate contained three delectable doughy confections piled with peaks of powdered sugar. A whiff of coffee hit Brad's nose. He drank till he felt the warmth reach his stomach then picked up the first of the *beignets*, savouring its moist, yeasty smell. Surprised to find his appetite kicking in, he indulged guiltily, wondering how long it was since Zach had eaten.

Before long, the tiles beneath his feet were covered in powdered sugar. There was really no way to eat this stuff without making a mess, so he simply gave up the fight and indulged himself.

With food in his stomach, Brad felt a little better and his mind a little clearer. As Pachelbel's long-winded canon seemed to be threading its way to a climax of sorts, he signalled his server. She scowled and held up an imperious finger— *Patience!*—then stomped back over to him. On the way, she brushed against a napkin holder on the edge of one of the tables, where it tottered briefly before crashing to the floor. Her eyes flared with indignation. She glared at Brad as though he were personally responsible not only for making her knock the napkin holder off the table, but for her shitty job as well.

"You want something else?" she asked in a tone that said he had better not.

"Just a cheque."

"Four dollars."

Brad gave her a five and told her to keep the change. She accepted the tip with zero-point-three seconds of a smile on one side of her mouth. Perhaps a full smile cost another dollar.

Brad left the café thinking only of Zach and how to find him. He wandered disconsolately, his footfalls echoing hollowly on the pavement until his stride took him down Pirate's Alley to a darkened laneway. Apart from a lone cab up ahead, the street was deserted. Most of the storefronts were boarded up. The others merely looked foreboding. One window display contained miniature replicas of civil war weapons—ancient canonry, muskets and soldiers. The sign overhead read, *Toys of Mass Destruction*.

Brad passed three small shops, each

185

proclaiming itself "The Only True Home" of the city's Voodoo culture, as though they were all engaged in some weird Voodoo Authenticity war. On the far side of the street, a man stopped and turned abruptly to look in a store window. But not before Brad saw that one side of his head was completely shaved. It was the man Hedy claimed had broken into her room the night before she was killed.

Before he could decide what to do, two more men rounded the corner and stood shoulder to shoulder with him. The newcomers were decked out in snazzy dress suits. Still, they looked as though they might be able to do some damage, given the choice. Brad wouldn't have been surprised if they carried guns, but didn't want to find out the hard way.

The man with the shaved head turned to look at him and the others followed suit. As one, they began to walk in his direction. Brad bolted, elated by the timely return of his powers of mobility. And not a moment too soon, he thought, as he rounded a corner and dashed out of sight.

He found himself in an empty alleyway. Up ahead, swinging from a link of chain, a hand-carved sign caught his eye. Wrapped in the coils of a menacing-looking snake was the name "Marie Laveau."

For a second, it didn't register. Suddenly, Brad recalled his nightmare vision of the mausoleums in the City of the Dead. The name "Marie Laveau" had clearly been imprinted on one of them. Now he knew why it had sounded so familiar: Laveau was the famed Voodoo queen that Zach had told him about.

He made a dash for the shop.

The door opened and closed behind him with a faint tinkle. Brad found himself wreathed in a cloud of incense. Curious, he thought, as he peered at an unruly display on the store's shelves. There were shrunken heads, coloured candles, bottles of oil, powders for luck, love and fertility, books of magic spells, amulets and trinkets, Voodoo dolls, snake skins, crows' feet, altars, incense, cowrie shells, starfish, rosaries, masks, and row upon row of Tarot cards. In fact, there was something to suit just about every fetish, spiritual or otherwise.

At the back of the shop, a woman with purple hair and luminous green eyes regarded him intently.

"Can I help you?"

"I'd like to see Marie, please."

She chuckled. "Good luck with that."

"I beg your pardon?"

"Marie Laveau died in 1881. Perhaps I can be of assistance. I'm Madame Leah, a spiritual descendant of Marie. But I make no claims. This is my shop."

"Oh," Brad said. "Well, here's the story: in about ten seconds, three very nasty men are going to come through that door looking for me. I don't really know why I'm here, but I dreamed about the name Marie Laveau. I was walking through this very strange place where everything was grey and—"

"City of the Dead?"

"How'd you know?"

"Just a guess."

The front door chime tinkled and Brad looked up as the shaved-headed man entered with his cronies behind him.

"Anyway, that would be them," he said.

Madame Leah glanced over at the men then turned her liquid gaze back on Brad. "I could give you a broom to fly away on, but there's no time to teach you how to use it." She put a finger to her lips. "Let me take care of this. I'll make you invisible."

She whirled in her chair and stood to face the newcomers. "Gentlemen!" she exclaimed. "Welcome to the House of Marie Laveau. We have everything for your occult needs. What's your preference—casting spells or removing them? White magic or the dirty, rotten scoundrel kind? Or are you perhaps just looking for a little touristy diversion here in the Big Easy?"

Brad watched curiously. Madame Leah's snake-oil salesman patter was accompanied by a series of hand gestures that seemed to mesmerize the newcomers.

"A little bit of quirk to scratch a curious itch? No? Then perhaps you're in search of a treatise on the origins of Baphomet or a genuine Haitian Voodoo party hat? Might I interest you in a veil from Our Lady of Guadalupe or an altar from a Mexican Day of the Dead ceremony? If you need an amulet to arm yourself against the plague or a magic sword to hex your mother-in-law, these too I can provide. Whatever you seek, I assure you that

I, Madame Leah, am at your service."

Brad had folded himself into a corner, though he was still in view of the entire shop. He watched the men intently. They suddenly seemed unsure why they were there. Better yet, they stopped looking around with murderous rage and were blinking in confused bewilderment.

Madame Leah kept up her patter until the men retreated, backing out the entrance and assuring her they'd come into the store by mistake. Was there a Hooters nearby, by any chance? The chime tinkled as they left. Madame Leah closed the door behind them and locked it with a dead bolt.

She whirled around to Brad. "So you've been to the City of the Dead?"

"It was just a dream I had."

"We all start somewhere. Come and sit."

She nodded to a table covered in burgundy velvet, waited till he'd seated himself and then gazed intently at him over a large crystal ball.

"Am I really invisible?" Brad asked. "I mean, it was as if those guys didn't even see me."

Madame Leah shook her head. A smile played across her lips. "Nah, not really," she said. "I didn't actually have time to make you invisible, so I made them think you were a ten-year-old skateboarder. Worked like a charm."

"Okay."

"You know how it is: if you want something badly enough and believe in it strongly enough, in a way it becomes real. Some call it wishful thinking. I call it magic. Whatever works."

Brad just nodded.

"Now, let's look into the ball to see if there's a message for you."

She hunched down and covered her brow with both hands, looking into the crystal and nodding as though she were agreeing with someone or something inside the ball. Then she snorted and looked up.

"What's it say?" Brad asked curiously.

"It says the one you seek is alive, but beware when you meet him again. It also says love will only break your heart and that you always hurt the one you love."

"I've heard that before."

Madame Leah looked off pensively. "Yeah, me too. It sounds like a Britney Spears song."

Brad shook his head. "No, I mean I've heard those exact words recently. Have you heard of Doctor Doom?"

Madame Leah's face was pure disgust. "Oh, that overrated piece of scrap metal!"

"He said exactly the same thing as you just now."

"Really? Well, sometimes he's not so bad."

"What does it mean?" Brad asked.

"I don't have a clue," she said with a shrug. "I don't interpret, I just repeat what I see and hear. I'm a psychic, not a psychiatrist."

"Is there anything else in there for me?"

Madame Leah turned back to the ball then said after a moment, "To find what you seek, you must go to the City of the Dead." She glanced up, a look of distress on her face. "I've never known anyone who went there who came back alive."

"I'd go to hell and back to find the one I love," Brad said.

Her gaze was distant, as though she'd gone into a trance. "You may have to," she murmured.

"Where do I find the City of the Dead?"

"First and foremost you must be prepared to find it in your mind, for it's a mental place as much as a physical one. But the entrance is material enough: it's the gate to the St. Louis Cemetery."

"What do I do?"

"Enter the graveyard by the main gate then make an immediate left and a sharp right. Walk up the narrow laneway between the crypts. They're above ground and stacked one on top of another to save space." She sighed. "Even in death, this city has a housing crisis on its hands. Anyway, walk till you find the tomb with the name Glapion on it. Near the bottom you'll see 'Marie, nee Laveau.' That's the party you want."

"No appointment necessary, I take it."

Madame Leah shook her head.

"The doctor will see you when the doctor will see you, and not a second before. Same old story." She shrugged. "Once you find her, pick up a stone from the ground—preferably an orange one if you can find it, but the tourists take them all. Mark an 'X' on the tomb. Call Marie's name aloud and say, 'I am here to ask for your help.' Then place your hand on the X, make your wish and rub your foot three times on the bottom of the crypt."

Bradford listened intently.

"Have you got that so far?"

He nodded furiously. "I've got it."

"Okay. If Marie is in a good mood, she'll answer you with a vision. Whatever happens, don't be afraid. Remember, it's only a vision. It can't hurt you. Once you've had your vision, remove your hand and make another X beside the first one. Then drop some silver coins into the jars around the base of the tomb and take your leave."

"And then?"

"Then go and live your life. Marie will answer your prayers when she's good and ready. Once you get your wish, go back and mark a third X beside the other two to note the debt paid. Only don't get caught doing any of this, because you'll be arrested for defacing city property."

Brad thought it over. "Should I go at any special time of night?" he asked.

Madame Leah laughed. "You mean like at the stroke of midnight?"

Brad nodded. "It just seems like a propitious time, from everything I've read."

She shook her head. "Nah—that's a bunch of crap. Just make sure it's dark. And watch out for those idiot Voodoo tours. Those guides make up half that garbage. They don't have a clue what they're talking about."

She looked over her shoulder and plucked a small object from a display shelf.

"Here—take this *gris-gris*. It will enhance your powers."

Brad looked at the small bundle of cloth tied in a string. Zach had mentioned a *gris-gris* in his discourse on zombies. He wished he'd paid more attention now.

"What's inside?"

"Bunch of chicken bones and a few coloured pebbles. Nothing to worry about or get you arrested. Least not in this town. It's the magic spell placed over it that helps more than the junk inside. That's just window dressing."

"How does it work?"

"Here's the deal: I can give you special powers, but they won't last long. It's your intention that makes things happen. You know what I mean?"

"I guess."

She held up a hand, splaying her fingers in a fanlike motion before folding them back into her palm. "Do this and picture a silver half moon followed by a vision of what you want in your mind's eye. If you successfully project the energy, it will happen. That's pretty much it."

"Okay."

"And hopefully that will do it. On the other hand, if you want to break a spell you need to get some pig bristles cooked at a Voodoo ritual. Tie them into a bundle and carry them with you at all times. Or if you want your lover to stay away from somebody else, put a drop of your blood in his coffee. Also, you can make a well go dry by dissolving soda in it every day for one week then drawing a bucket of water out and throwing it on the earth."

"Wow—something for every occasion."

"Oh, yeah. We got all kinds of cool stuff in here."

"How can I thank you?"

"Keep the faith." Madame Leah smiled. "And try to come back alive. Good luck!"

Leaving the shop, Brad was nearly knocked flat by a gangly teenager on a skateboard with a rat tail of hair flying in the wind behind him.

"Lookout, dude!" was the extent of his growled warning.

Bradford threw his hands out unconsciously in a semblance of the move Madame Leah had shown him in the shop a minute earlier. "I'd like to see that little skank go flying," he thought, pressing himself against a wall to avoid getting run over.

The kid whisked by. Brad watched as the boy approached the intersection, only to find himself heading straight for an oncoming car. He shouted at the driver much as he'd shouted at Bradford, though this time his warning had less of an effect. He swerved at the last moment, his skateboard flying out from beneath him. Brad suppressed a grin as he walked past the kid, who lay in the dirt rubbing an elbow.

"What are you laughing at, dickhead?" the twerp dared to ask.

"Justice served," Bradford answered, and walked on.

Not bad, he thought, reflecting on the hand gesture and Madame Leah's explanation of making intentions reality. If something like that happens again, I might just start believing in this Voodoo stuff.

18

Brad was relieved to see Quint standing inside the gate when he returned to the Lion's Roar. He'd worried about the boy the entire time he was away—when he wasn't focused on finding Zach. If the police had released him then it was good news. At the very least, it meant they had insufficient evidence to keep him locked up.

"Hi, Quint. Good to see you back again."

Quint stared mournfully at Bradford. He seemed chastened by whatever he'd gone through while he was away. "Ah don't like the big, wide world," he said.

"It's a common reaction."

The boy squinted up at the sky. "That big yellow ball is kindly to us today."

"It's called the 'sun,' Quint."

Quint looked at him curiously. "The sun?"

Brad nodded.

"Ah'm a son," Quint said.

"Different kind of sun," Bradford said, recalling the woman who thought she had recognized him. "Do you remember whose son you are, Quint?"

"Surely," Quint replied. "Ah am the son of Dog. Dog looks after his own. He loves us all."

"I think you mean 'God'," Bradford said. "God looks after His own."

"Surely."

Brad wondered what backwoods religion had warped this boy's mind. "Do you remember where you came from, Quint?"

"From the garden. We all come from the garden, Bradford."

"Did you like it there? Was it a nice garden?" Brad asked.

A frown crossed Quint's face. He looked warily off to the gate. "Sometimes it was nice, but not always."

Just then Derek emerged from the inn. "Any news of Zach?" he asked.

Brad shook his head. "No."

"Sorry to hear it."

"Thank you. I intend to keep searching for him."

"Anything you need from us, just ask."

"Will do."

"And if you don't mind my saying so, you're looking a little rough," Derek said. "And I'm being very polite when I say 'rough.' I still think you had better see a doctor."

"It's been a long night," Bradford said. "I was just telling Quint how glad I am to see him back."

"I surely am glad to be here with Philip and Derek," Quint said. "They are good to me."

Derek smiled congenially. "Quint, could you go check to see if the pool needs skimming while I talk with Brad?"

"Sure thing, Derek," Quint said, and walked off.

"Poor kid," Brad said when Quint had gone. "He's had a hard time."

Looking over his shoulder at Quint, Derek dropped his voice. "He was lucky. His prints weren't on the knife. There were others, though, and bloody ones at that. The police dropped Quint off yesterday when he told them he didn't know how to get back to the inn. I think they finally believed our story that he is just a simple kid who was trying to comfort Hedy as she lay dying."

"And do you?" Brad asked, watching Derek intently.

Derek gave him a startled look. "I did until you asked me that. Why?"

"I'm just wondering why even a simple-minded kid would say things like 'that big yellow ball' when referring to the sun. Wouldn't even a simpleton know a word like 'sun'?"

Derek hesitated. "I've noticed his many oddities, but never thought too deeply about them before. I just assumed he'd been traumatized by the beating he received before he got here. Don't they say that one side of the brain controls word usage? Maybe that's the side that got damaged in the fight."

Brad looked over to where Quint was skimming the pool with a long-handled net. "You might be right," he said. "He seems to get words and phrases backwards. It would make perfect sense if it was from a head injury."

He paused.

197

"But...?" Derek said.

"I don't know. I just get the feeling a whole lot more is going on here than meets the eye."

Derek scuffed the tiles at his feet. "I wish I could tell you what that is."

"Any news on Mr. Sakamoto and Mr. Nobutsugo?"

Derek shook his head. "They haven't returned since they left yesterday morning, right before the murder was discovered. I checked their room. All their belongings are still there. It's like they've just abandoned everything. Philip and I are trying to appear cooperative with the police, so we let them know. They're coming by this afternoon to dust their room for prints to see if they match the prints on the knife."

He hesitated, a grim look on his usually imperturbable features.

"Don't tell me—they want to dust my room for my prints too.

Derek nodded sheepishly.

"Then let them in. It's your duty." Brad put an arm around Derek's shoulder. "I'm sorry. This must be hard on both of you."

Derek straightened. "Stiff upper lip and all that rot. I'm not an Englishman for nothing, you know."

Brad finally let Derek and Philip convince him to go to the hospital. They drove him there and waited while tests were done. A friendly doctor gave him a thorough going-over. The results showed no major trauma. Back at the inn, his hosts convinced Brad to lie down and rest, reassuring him they would be alert for any calls or news of any sort.

He spent the afternoon in bed. When he woke again, the sun had set below the rooftops. He dressed and went out to the pool, deserted now in the early evening light. He knelt and trailed a hand in the water, scooping up handfuls of the cool wetness and letting it fall back onto the surface with a splat.

The dogs were lolling around the courtyard, little clowns of friendly devotion. Miss Muffet had her nose up Mr. Tuffet's bum, while Lola and Digger Dog were having a skirmish over nothing. Brad thought how different they were from the Doberman that attacked him and Zach at the warehouse. Derek and Philip's mutts weren't trained guard dogs, of course, but Brad wondered just what it would take for them to attack an intruder as Gumbo had. To what degree were behaviour patterns already programmed into an animal's genetic code and simply lying in wait for the switch to be flipped to turn a loving pet into a terrifying killer?

Derek arrived with a tray of food. Brad took a few exploratory bites, but his mind was elsewhere. He lay by the pool a long time wondering what was happening with Zach, wherever he was. He attempted one of Zach's Remote Viewing exercises, which his partner claimed was nothing more than meditation, blanking his mind and waiting for whatever images and feelings came in to fill the void. He simply felt numb. Numb and cold and dark, as if he were inside a refrigerator. Not much use in that, he thought, dismissing the idea.

Night came on, slowly filling the sky with stars like pinprick holes in a roof. The pool twinkled and rippled in the dreamy darkness. For the next little while, there was nothing to do but wait.

Several hours later, his pockets filled with silver coins and unconsciously fingering the *gris-gris*, Bradford made his way across town to the St. Louis Cemetery. Every step he took was heavy with dread. Dread of what he would find in the City of the Dead, dread that he would never see Zach again and, in the back of his mind, dread that he himself might never return once he'd entered those mysterious gates.

Despite what Madame Leah had said to pooh-pooh any particular hour being better than another for magic ceremonies, it was just this side of midnight when Brad approached the cemetery. Not unexpectedly, a heavy chain lay wrapped around the handles of the main entrance.

"Now what?" he wondered, reaching out to shake the lock.

He recalled Madame Leah's injunction about belief and intention. He held up his hands, fanning his fingers while envisioning a silver half moon and imagining the lock falling to the ground. He added a grunt for good measure, as though to dramatize how much effort he was putting into his intention.

Good intentions notwithstanding, the chain remained securely fastened. Brad rattled it in annoyance, as though it had violated some sacred command. He even grunted a second time, letting the heavy lock fall back against the gate with a resounding clank.

Five yards away, a smaller gate he'd overlooked earlier swung open to emit a pair of visitors to the cemetery grounds. Bradford stared as the men emerged, outfitted in black leather, and with multiple chains attached to various orifices, as though they'd just been ejected from a Mr. Leatherman contest. One of them looked at Brad and shook his head.

"Crappy tour, man," he said. "The Lesbian Vampire Tour was much better than this shit."

Brad shook his head. "Uh, pizza delivery only," he said.

Seeing the men's confused looks, he realized he wasn't holding a pizza box. "Erm, pick-up, that is. Pizza pick-up. Excuse me," he said, brushing past them and into the grounds.

The cemetery was quite unlike most other cemeteries. Just as Madame Leah had described, the tombs were layered in oven-like configurations, as though multiple levels of baking were going on at any given time. Rather than looking down at the graves, Bradford felt dwarfed by the stone edifices that towered over him like miniature buildings—the same buildings he'd seen in his dream.

As instructed, he turned left then made an immediate right. Up ahead, a crowd brandishing candles and talking in excited whispers gathered around a particular tomb. That, he guessed, would be the tomb of Marie Laveau, famed Voodoo queen of New Orleans.

Brad approached quietly and stood off to one side not to disturb them. He listened to the guide's somnolent voice as it unfurled creepy tales of the living dead and ghosts who returned from the next world to carry loved ones back to shadowy realms. The guys in leather were right: it was a crappy tour, one that would impress only the most unimaginative and gullible.

"And if you all don't tip me proper and good when this tour ends, Marie Laveau will curse you all the way she cursed all her enemies and made them die horrible deaths, one by one," said the guide.

And no doubt you've already fleeced these poor suckers into paying you a sizeable sum to listen to this nonsense, Bradford thought. The huckster didn't even have a proper N'Orleans accent.

The guide's voice halted in its rhythmic unfolding of witchery and black arts. "And then there's always some cheap asshole like that guy standing over there in the shadows"—at this the entire tour turned to regard Bradford—"who done thinks it's fine to cheat a hard-working, legitimately-trained tour guide out of his rightful fee."

Brad wondered if he should slink away rather than face embarrassment. He was about to explain that he was just waiting his turn to visit the tomb when the guide said, "And don't give me some horseshit about you ain't trying to overhear my secrets, 'cause I know you is."

Brad couldn't resist. "Well, you is wrong," he said. "And don't give me some horseshit about how

202

you is trying to speak in a N'Orleans dialect, 'cause you ain't."

"I curse you, man," the guide said. "I throw a big fat Voodoo curse on you to leave this place right now."

The image of a half moon formed in Brad's head. He fanned his fingers as Madame Leah had taught him, imagining the guide falling flat on his face like the skateboarder who'd been knocked over earlier in the day.

On seeing Brad's hand movements, the guide laughed out loud. "Don't pull that Voodoo shit on me. Tell Madame Leah I got bigger magic," he said boastfully, as he turned and walked smack into a tomb.

Some of the tourists giggled. The guide whirled on them angrily.

"You all wanna watch I don't curse you for the rest of your life," he warned, as they trooped off to another part of the graveyard.

Brad waited till their footsteps faded then moved closer to the brickwork. Even in the dark he could make out a myriad of X's in groups of twos and threes, covering the tomb from top to bottom. Marie's been busy, he thought. He stooped and picked up a stone he hoped was orange, despite the darkness.

Reaching out, he made a bold criss-cross on the stone.

"I call on the Voodoo queen Marie Laveau," he said. "I, Bradford Fairfax, request her assistance."

With one hand on the tomb, he made his wish. Wishes being what they are, they may not be spoken aloud or written down in books like this one for fear of ruining them, but it should not be hard to imagine what Brad might have been wishing for so fervently on that particular evening just past midnight in the St. Louis Cemetery.

He waited a second then carefully rubbed the bottom of the tomb with his shoe. Nothing happened. For a moment, Brad wondered if he should have used his other foot or maybe worn different shoes. He opened his eyes and looked around. Nothing had changed. Maybe he needed to concentrate harder.

He closed his eyes again and repeated his wish. Seconds passed, turning into a full minute. He was growing impatient when suddenly from nowhere a ghostly tiger, its irises glittering, leapt directly at him. Brad let out a shout and opened his eyes, stumbling backwards. He was still there, safe and sound in the cemetery at fifteen minutes past the hour of midnight, with no tigers in sight. Embarrassed, he recalled Leah's words: *Remember, it's only a vision. It can't hurt you.*

He took a deep breath, mustering the courage to return to that netherworld. Slowly, he reached out a hand and placed it against the X, determined to go through with it and enter the City of the Dead. This time he warned himself not to flinch or turn away, no matter how terrifying the vision.

Eyes closed, he once again found himself within the bounds of that dismal grey city he'd glimpsed in his dreams. It looked just like the cemetery he stood in, with the same miniature houses lining the roads, only it was changed somehow. He could see the same strange shadows shifting around him, but now he knew them for what they were: the shadows of invisible spirits who once, but no longer, were men.

A wolf-like howling filled the air. Faceless creatures approached, their bluish skin giving off an icy hue. Brad felt the same terror he'd had on seeing the boys snap the man's neck back at the warehouse. He darted and ducked as they threw themselves at him, snarling and foaming at the mouth, though his mind solidly refuted what he was seeing. Each time the creatures grabbed at him, their arms seemed to go right through him. In this underworld of darkness and confusion, it was as though he were the insubstantial being and not them.

Suddenly, as if cued, the slathering wraiths withdrew. A new figure appeared, walking toward him down the long narrow lanes of the cemetery. Brad's heart beat wildly. What had Madame Leah and Doctor Doom said? *The one you seek is alive, but beware when you meet him again.*

Brad steeled himself. He was here to retrieve Zach from the City of the Dead and return him to the world of the living. Nothing else mattered. Madame Leah had said that reality was merely a matter of belief. If he held fast to his conviction then he and Zach would walk out of this nightmare zone of fiendish shadows and zombie-like ghouls together. Then again, Madame Leah had also said she'd never known anyone to return from that place alive.

The figure had almost reached him. Shadows

obscured its face, but even in shadow Brad could make out Zach's familiar features. The figure stopped, eyeing Brad warily. There was a bluish hue to its skin.

Brad stretched out a hand. "Zach," he said. "It's me, Bradford."

Instead of replying, Zach snarled like a rabid dog and leapt straight at Brad, fangs bared and claws outstretched.

Brad's eyes flew open. The vision vanished. Unbelievably, he was still in the cemetery standing alone beside Marie Laveau's tomb. The spell had been broken. Zach was gone.

"Noooooo!" he howled at the empty sky.

He closed his eyes again, desperate to recapture what he'd lost and will himself back to that place, no matter what might happen to him.

Nothing. The vision was gone.

He'd failed utterly.

After fifteen minutes of trying to return to the City of the Dead, he gave up. It was futile.

He was about to leave when he recalled the final part of the instructions. Retracing his steps to Marie Laveau's tomb, he made a second criss-cross beside the first. He'd had his vision, after all. Then he emptied his pockets into the cups. Heartbroken, he retreated back to the Lion's Roar, hoping for the forgiving graces of sleep.

19

Brad woke to feelings of exhaustion and despair. It was now more than thirty-six hours since he'd seen Zach—at least since he'd seen Zach in the flesh, if you didn't count the encounter with the man-eating ghouls in the cemetery. An overwhelming sense of loss and dread had fuelled his dreams all night long, leaving him with an even greater sense of urgency to find his lover. The only problem was, he'd run out of places to look.

He checked his cell phone. There were three messages: two from DC Beaulieu and one from Grace. He'd missed them all while he'd been soundly asleep—or perhaps, he might say, while he'd slept like the dead.

He dialled Grace first, but got no answer. If she was looking for an update, there wasn't much to report other than a midnight visit to the tomb of a Voodoo queen that had made him feel even more helpless than before. He left a message saying he'd heard nothing further from Agent Kong then hung up and called Beaulieu. At the police station, a weary voice told him that Officer Beaulieu was tied up in meetings and would get back to him when he could.

There was nothing else to do but go back to where he'd last seen Zach and start looking again. Derek and Philip offered to join him but he refused, unwilling to put them at further risk. Over the next few hours and well into the afternoon he repeated the previous day's search, scouring the derelict buildings down by the waterfront. They seemed eerily empty. Nor was there any no sign of Zach or the savage pack of boys. Brad wondered where they holed up during the day, since they seemed active mostly at night.

His wanderings eventually brought him back to the abandoned train yard. He shielded his eyes from the sun and looked across the dried fields. From a distance, the upraised palm of Doctor Doom seemed once again to be waving to him. Time for another check-up with the good doctor, he told himself.

He scouted the deserted lot. So far as he could see, there were no dogs of any variety waiting for the chance to rip his throat out. As he approached the caretaker's office, he could make out voices coming from inside. Perhaps some desperate soul was there to seek the doctor's wisdom.

"Ah'm just checking to make sure things are going well here. Any problems, you let us know at once," someone said.

"Oh, y-y-yes, sir," replied a voice Brad knew belonged to the meek little rabbit who kept track of the doctor's appointments.

"I'll be back at midnight. Ah've got a job for you."

"B-b-but the demons c-c-come at night!"

So he knew about the marauding band of killers!

"Nonsense. There are no demons. That's just superstitious mumbo-jumbo. Ah'll be back tonight. You all better be here."

"Y-y-yes, sir."

Brad ducked around a corner as the door flew open and footsteps crunched across the gravel. He peered out from behind the building in time to see a tall figure with one side of his head shaved. Brad recognized him instantly as the man who'd followed him to Madame Leah's and the same man Hedy said broke into her room.

Just then Brad slipped on a loose stone. He pulled back, his heart pounding as the figure whirled, drew a gun and crouched low. Nothing happened. After thirty tension-filled seconds, he peered around the wall to see the man striding across the far end of the deserted lot.

Once the killer was out of sight, Brad headed for the office. The meek little man looked up in fright as he entered.

"I'll do whatever you s-s-say..." he began, then stopped and regarded Brad with a cross between fear and surprise.

"Oh, it's you. I'm s-s-sorry, sir, but we are c-c-closed today," he said, as Brad headed for the door to the doctor's office.

"Your sign says 'Open,'" Brad told him.

"You can't go in there without an ap-p-pointment," the little man stuttered. "Doctor Doom w-w-will be very angry!"

"I'll deal with it," Brad said, yanking the door open.

As usual, the room was dark and cool. Brad grabbed the curtains and yanked them aside. Doctor Doom stood mutely before him, its contours shrouded in shadows.

"Who was that man who was just here?" Brad demanded, examining the silent machine.

"Oh, m-m-my. I'm in such a state! I don't want to annoy those m-m-men. They are very desperate. I'm afraid of w-w-what they will do to me."

"What do they want?"

The man's face fell. "They want to repossess the f-f-franchise. They say they're going to t-t-tear down these warehouses and build a new condominium c-c-complex."

He shivered.

"He's a real estate developer?" Brad demanded.

"Y-y-yes!"

"Why is he returning tonight at midnight?"

"I don't know! But I c-c-can't be here! The demons come out at n-n-night."

"What are these demons?" Brad asked. "I've seen them too."

"P-p-pure evil," said the little man. "Doctor Doom p-p-predicted it. It's God's handiwork. This is His way of d-d-dealing with the sin and degradation that has descended upon our good and f-f-fair city."

"Oh, cut it out," Brad said. "No one ever called New Orleans 'good' or 'fair.' And don't tell me all despots get what's coming to them. Otherwise, George W. Bush and Saddam Hussein would have had their comeuppance by now."

His phone rang. It was Beaulieu.

"Is this the self-appointed saviour of N'Orleans?" said the DC's gravelly voice.

Brad cut through the cop's sarcasm. "What do you want, Beaulieu?"

"Don't git yer danders up. Ah'm phoning to give y'all a little tip," the officer told him. "Ah am only doing it because your information turned something up and ah said ah'd share."

"I'm all ears," Brad said. "Fill me in."

"First off, we found the body with a broken neck right where y'all said." The cop paused. "Of course, that makes y'all prime suspect number one."

"I'll deal with that if I have to," Brad said. "What else did you find?"

"It turns out Chester Morgenstern is the name of a real person, jest like y'all said. While ah cain't say for sure it's your boy Quint, ah can say Chester Morgenstern is listed as having gone missing in Katrina."

Not exactly burning news, thought Bradford. "So it's very possible that they are one and the same."

"Yes," said Beaulieu.

"Any criminal record for Chester?"

"None. And while it would be convenient to compare fingerprints of the two, we don't have Morgenstern's prints to compare with your boy's."

"What about DNA?"

"We're workin' on it. It could take some time."

"What about family? Any clue to their

whereabouts? Maybe you could show them Quint's photograph."

"The Morgensterns are a family of up-standing reputation in N'Orleans. Chester Morgenstern's father is the Right Reverend Septimus Morgenstern of the Tabernacle of the True Vine."

Bells were ringing loudly in Brad's ears: *I am the true vine, and my Father is the gardener.*

"What? Did y'all say something'?"

"Yes," Brad replied. "I said, thank you. I'm very pleased to hear it."

He hung up and looked at the little man, who cowered at his glance.

"Do you remember the blue-haired young man who was here with me several days ago?" Bradford asked.

The mouse nodded. "Y-y-yes. Mr. Kong. If I'm n-n-not mistaken."

"That's him. He's missing and might be in trouble. If he shows up here or if you see any sign of him, please call this number immediately."

Brad handed him a card. The little man looked at it carefully.

"All right," he said.

"And watch out for those demons," Brad told him. "They're killers."

"I know," said the man, his eyes wide in consternation.

Brad left the office and strode back to the Lion's Roar. He found Quint in the courtyard skimming the pool.

"Hello, Mr. Bradford," the boy said dolefully.

"Hello, Quint," Brad replied, his mind racing.

212

How much did this boy really know and how much might it be safe to reveal to him? "Do you remember our conversation earlier when I asked if you knew whose son you were?"

"Surely," Quint said. "Ah am Dog's son."

"True enough. Do you remember a church, Quint? Do you recall a church called the Tabernacle of the True Vine?"

Quint looked at him warily and nodded. "The vine that grows in the garden. We must all tend the true vine. It is a mighty oak," he said, as though reciting some proverb he'd been taught in Sunday school. He frowned. "We're not supposed to leave the garden."

"You won't have to," Brad said. "I'm bringing the garden to you." He paused. "I'd tell you not to go anywhere, but I'm pretty sure that won't be necessary."

A perplexed look crossed Quint's face as Bradford left again, the gate banging loudly behind him.

Brad reached the Tabernacle of the True Vine in record speed. He stood regarding the sign with the day's sermon on it: "Weeding the Evil Demons and Boll Weevils from God's Garden."

Another sure-fire ecclesiastical hit, Brad thought. Such a joyful bunch, these evangelicals.

Inside, the reverend was preaching to the usual sorry-looking louts and wastrels, delivering a sermon no doubt intended to rescue all his listeners from whatever soul-damaging fun or joy they might be contemplating.

"We must continue God's handiwork," he

roared, like a man possessed. "He hath rooted out the evil that liveth in the garden. He hath routed the heathens and infidels. And now it's time for us to continue His handiwork!"

God's handiwork! Brad was not oblivious to that particular phrasing. Hedy had said it was in the letter from her husband to her former boss.

The reverend glanced up in surprise as Brad came storming down the aisle, pointing a finger at him.

"What in God's name—?"

"I command you in the name of God to stop this fear mongering and follow me," Brad shouted.

Anger flashed across the reverend's features. "Ah know you, sir. You are a miserable sinner. Do not take the Lord's name in vain!"

"I am come to deliver your only begotten son, Chester Morgenstern."

"You will not—!" The man faltered. "My son?" he cried. "You know where my son is?"

"I do," Brad said. "And I will take you to him if you come with me right now."

"But how—?"

"Now!" Bradford commanded.

The pastor looked around at his sorry congregation then stepped down off the pulpit.

"If this is a joke..." he began.

"I assure you, this is no joke," Brad told him.

"Then lead me to him," he said, all pomposity deflated.

The old man was silent in the cab on the way to the Lion's Roar. Brad explained how he got involved with his son, who seemed to be suffering from amnesia, and of the woman who thought she recognized him. He did not bring up the residual charge of murder, as he thought it might prove somewhat of a deterrent at present.

When they reached the inn, Brad paid and the pair got out of the cab. The reverend stopped on the sidewalk looking worriedly through the gate.

"Are you sure...?" he began.

Brad saw fear written on the man's face. "I know you have no reason to trust me," he began.

"It's not that," the man said apprehensively. "I ... I don't want to be disappointed again."

Brad nodded. "I pray I'm not getting your hopes up in vain, but you'll just have to come in and meet him and see for yourself."

"Just ... give me one minute," said the reverend.

"I'll go prepare Chester," Brad told him, slipping through the gate. "You come when you're ready."

As Brad approached the courtyard, he heard something scurrying through the garden.

"Quint," he called softly. "It's me, Bradford."

The greenery parted and Quint stepped out of the bushes.

"Hi, Mister Bradford," he said. "Ah was afraid. Ah heard a noise at the gate to the big, wide world."

"That was me. And a friend. I've brought someone to visit you, Quint," Brad told him.

"Take care!" Quint's face betrayed fear. "Quint doesn't want to see a friend."

"It's all right," Brad told him. "He won't hurt

you."

Footsteps approached. The boy tried to bolt, but Brad grabbed hold of his hand. He felt the chill in his grip.

"Please, Quint, It's all right. Just hold my hand."

Brad turned to see the Right Reverend Septimus Morgenstern approaching the courtyard. On seeing Quint, the reverend's face crumpled. He was overcome with emotion. For a moment, a wild grief shone in the old man's eyes.

"Son?" he said faintly. "Is it really you come back to us?"

"Ah am a son," Quint replied.

"Dare I hope?" Septimus asked, reaching out a hand.

Quint stood there, curious, as the fingers played on his cheek, softly caressing the skin.

"Chester, is it really you?"

The hand suddenly recoiled and the reverend's expression hardened. He looked down at his fingers, as though they'd been burned. He whirled on Bradford.

"This is not my son!"

"Are you sure?" Brad asked, hoping the man would change his mind.

Anger flared in the reverend's eyes. "And you, sir, are an agent of the devil." The reverend turned back to Quint. "Demon! Get thee behind me!"

Quint regarded him curiously. "Ah'm not a demon," he said softly. "Mah name is Quint. Ah am a son."

Bradford watched in bewilderment as the

reverend stormed out of the courtyard and down the walk, letting the gate slam behind him. He waited a moment then turned to Quint.

"I'm sorry, Quint," he said. "I thought he might have known you. Did you recognize him?"

"No." Quint shook his head. "Was he your father?"

"No," Bradford said. "Not mine. He's not anybody's father, apparently."

20

Brad was as bewildered as anybody about what was going on in New Orleans. A well-intentioned do-gooder had been murdered when she tried to meddle in the city's reconstruction process, Zach had disappeared while investigating her murder, and now two guests of the inn had vanished. What, if anything, linked the incidents was anybody's guess. All Brad knew was that there was a meeting scheduled at Doctor Doom's at midnight, and he was going to be in on it.

There was no one in sight as he crept across the darkened field to the doctor's office. No light showed from inside. Perhaps the little man had found the backbone to make good his vow not to attend the get-together or maybe the realtors had already concluded their business with him and left. Whichever it was, Bradford was taking no chances on getting caught by the shaved-headed man and his dapper cronies or by the marauding gang of youthful killers.

The front door was ajar. Brad pushed it open and entered. Low voices came from the other room. He warily made his way inside the cool antechamber. The place was empty. Doctor Doom was gone. Even the curtains had been removed.

The talking continued as Brad made his way along to a small back room. The door was open. Inside, he saw the little man tied to a chair. The shaved-headed man leaned over him holding a gun to his head.

"You have two choices," he said. "Either I leave here with the signed deeds to the property or you leave here with a hole in your head."

"This is c-c-completely offensive," the little man spat out, pretty much stating the obvious, as far as Brad could see.

"Like it or not, my partners and I will have this property. Do you want the signature on the deed to be real or forged?"

"All r-r-right, I'll sign," the little man said.

The shaved-headed man loosened his bonds and the little man took the pen offered, putting his signature to paper. Done, the other folded the document and put it in his pocket.

"A wise choice," he said. "I'll leave you to untie yourself. By the time you do, the money transfer will have been made to your account. Half a million, as agreed. That will make things legal."

Just then a howl split the air right outside the office.

The shaved-headed man looked up. "What is that ungodly noise?"

"A l-l-little surprise," said the other.

"I hate surprises," said his captor, pocketing his gun and heading for the door. "Adiós, amigo," he said sarcastically.

"V-v-vaya con Dios, you mean," said the little man.

Brad withdrew into the shadows as the shaved-headed man walked past him and out the door.

Outside, the man stopped to light a cigarette and look around him. Shadowy forms flitted just outside the perimeter of light, waiting for his next move.

"Faggots!" Brad heard him curse under his breath.

The shaved-headed man headed across the empty field, disregarding the shadowy figures.

"Don't," Brad called out. "You're risking your life."

The man turned and regarded Brad. "You!" he cried. "Well, you're too late. I got what I wanted!"

"Don't go any further," Brad said. "Those things are killers. You'll regret it!"

"Another lunatic," said the man. "Besides, I got a gun."

Brad watched as he turned and continued across the field. Within seconds, he was surrounded by the pack of boys, who began to caress and kiss him.

"Let go, faggots!" he cried, as they crowded around.

It was too late. He was outnumbered. Brad slipped inside and shut the door as he heard a telltale snapping.

By the time he got to the smaller room, the little man had freed himself.

"Too l-l-late?" he asked.

"I tried to warn him," Brad said.

"He was t-t-too stupid to listen," said the other, petulantly.

"What happened here?"

"They've taken Doctor Doom," said the little man. "They m-m-made me sign a deed giving them ownership of these lands."

"Well, I don't think you'll have to worry about it for now," Brad said. "That deed didn't make it very far."

"Good!" said the little man. "Serves him right."

A trifle uncharitable, but not incorrect, Brad thought.

The little man rushed into the other room and surveyed the empty space where Doctor Doom used to sit.

"Oh, m-my," he said. "Whatever w-w-will I do without Doctor Doom?"

"You could always sell this land. Apparently it's worth half a million dollars."

"Never!" cried the caretaker. "Doctor Doom would never allow it. Doctor Doom will be very angry when he returns."

"Suit yourself."

Brad glanced out the window. The marauding tribe had gone off elsewhere. There was no sign of a body outside the window. He presumed they'd dragged it off with them.

"Are you l-l-leaving?" the little man cried.

"I'm going," Brad said.

The little man cringed. "I wouldn't go out there."

"You don't have to. I'll leave it up to you if you want to call the police. Take my word for it, though—they won't be in any hurry to investigate."

Brad's mind was in a whirl as he headed across the deserted grounds. He was sure he'd never find Zach now, if he was even alive. He'd also never solve Hedy's murder either. He'd been an utter failure at everything. It was in this despairing state that he found himself stumbling along the darkened streets. Before he realized it, he made one wrong turn and then another, before finding himself in the rollicking mania of Bourbon Street. From a distance, he heard a slithery beat. He looked up and saw the flickering lights of a marquee: "Harlan Masterson—Gentleman Stripper." His feet drew him inside and up the stairs where Harlan was just beginning his routine.

Brad ordered a bourbon and sat.

Half an hour later, his routine finished for the night, Harlan emerged from the dressing room and sat beside him.

"Thought I saw you out here, Red."

Brad looked up and nodded.

"What brings you out all by yourself? Not a fight with the boyfriend, I hope?" Harlan asked.

On his fourth bourbon by then, Brad shook his head morosely. For a moment, he thought he might cry. Taking care to be circumspect about certain salient facts, he began to let it out: Hedy's murder, the evening at the warehouse, the lethal cruising ground, Zach's disappearance. Harlan listened with rapt attention.

By the time he'd finished his tale, the bar lights began to flicker, signalling closing time.

"I'll help you, buddy. Whatever you need, but I doubt there's much that can be done about it tonight," Harlan told him.

"Jush as well," Brad said. "I'm a li'l tired."

"Time to leave," Harlan said. "Will you be able to make it home all right? I can take you back to my place, if you like."

"I'm fine," Brad said.

His legs suddenly gave out and he found himself on the floor. Harlan reached down and hauled him to his feet, but Brad was too wobbly to walk.

Harlan shook his head. "You big, sloppy beauty," he said, picking Brad up and slinging him over his shoulder. "You're coming home with me, buddy."

Outside, Harlan hailed a cab. The driver looked dubiously at the cowboy with the unconscious man slung over his shoulder.

"I'll give you two choices," Harlan said. "He can lie on the backseat with me or I'll toss him in the trunk, whatever you like. But if you want this fare, he's coming with me."

The driver laughed and they were soon heading to Harlan's hotel, without another peep from Brad.

Morning light is harsh in New Orleans, especially when it finds you lying unclothed on a bed in a strange hotel room. Brad woke with a massive headache and an even-more massive erection. Luckily enough, he had made it to a bed at least. Looking around further, he saw that he was lying beside a naked god.

Harlan's eyes flickered open. He reached over and rubbed Brad's tummy then kissed him.

"Good morning, Red."

Brad unstuck his tongue from the roof of his mouth. "Cetho ... sta ... hynbr..."

"This is the Olivier House, in case you're wondering, good buddy."

Harlan sprang out of bed and stretched in the morning light. Brad looked over the impeccable body.

"Did I...? Did we...?"

Harlan grinned. "Nah. I'm sure I would've enjoyed it for old times' sakes, but I didn't want to take advantage of you. Besides, with a cutie like that blue-haired boy what do you need with an old guy like me?"

"Not that it would matter to him. Zach didn't—doesn't—worry about such things."

"He's not the jealous type?"

Brad shook his head. "What we have is powerful, but it has nothing to do with ownership."

"That's enviable," Harlan said. "Whenever someone starts to get too attached and I hear the sound of wedding bells, I start feeling like a piece of real estate. When people say they want to marry you, what they mean is they want to own you. It's one of the reasons I never settled down."

"That and your wandering lasso, no doubt," Brad said.

"That too."

"I suppose we've got a lot of catching up to do," Brad said, wondering what he might have revealed the previous evening under the influence of too much bourbon and a massive bout of despair.

Harlan nodded. "True, though you did quite a bit of talking last night. Interesting how things have turned out for you..." The statement was left hanging in the air. "So, I guess your priority right now is to find that sweet little blue-haired boy of yours."

"Oh. I told you about that."

"Yup. And the sooner we start looking the better, I'd say. As I promised you last night—in case you don't remember—I will do anything I can to help you find him."

"Really?"

"Really, buddy. I meant it."

"I ... I don't know what I'd do without him."

He stopped short of saying he would quit the service if anything happened to Zach, because of course Harlan had no idea of Box 77 and everything that Brad had been up to in the last five years. It wouldn't do to reveal any trade secrets now.

For a second, Brad wondered whether he should tell Harlan what he and Zach were really doing the night Zach disappeared, though it occurred to him he could just take Harlan up on his offer for help without letting him know everything, so long as he didn't endanger him in the process. But telling the truth about Box 77 was *verboten!*

In fact, the only time Brad had revealed his true identity to anyone, the recipient of that information got the stupid idea in his head to join

Box 77, and he eventually did. That person was Zach. If Brad ever worried that he might one day regret his decision to tell Zach what he really did, that day was now. No—he wouldn't have a repeat of the situation. Not that Harlan was the type. For one thing, he was too sensible. For another, he was old enough to know better than to fantasize about running around the world doing good deeds to help others. And why would he, when his strip act already helped untold thousands of gay men get through their lives one day at a time.

"So..." Harlan said slowly. "This secret organization you belong to...?"

Brad gulped. "Secret organization?"

"You don't remember making me swear not to tell anyone?"

Brad shook his head.

"Box 77, right?"

Brad nodded. "I told you?"

Harlan was sheepish. "Yeah, kind of."

"Great," Brad said. "No need to torture Agent Red. Just give him a few glasses of bourbon and he'll tell all."

Harlan was watching him. "So? What's it really like being a secret agent?"

Brad cocked his head. "It's all right, except sometimes people try to kill you."

"I guess that's why you're in the spot you're in right now," Harlan offered.

Bradford's face fell. "If I don't find Zach, I don't know what I'll do."

"Then let's do whatever needs doing to find him," Harlan said, looking Brad in the eye. "And that is my most sincere offer, friend."

Brad took Harlan's hand and squeezed. Some had family, others had friends. Still others simply had blood bonds made in their formative years that for one reason or other remained among the most meaningful of relationships, even decades later.

A plan started to form in Brad's head. If he could get Harlan to help yet still keep him out of the way before things got dangerous, then they could go down to the waterfront and search for Zach together. If they encountered the gang of killer punks while they scoured the warehouses, he could use someone to distract them. As long as there was no risk to Harlan, it would work. It didn't take long for him to come up with a scheme.

21

That evening, well past the witching hour, two attractive, well-built men made their way along the banks of the Mississippi carrying a heavy burlap bag. One was a secret agent, the other a world-class stripper. The bag contained fireworks, but the fourth of July was still a long ways off.

Brad was grateful for Harlan's help, but he was also concerned about bringing an unknown into the equation. Although he knew Harlan could look after himself under normal circumstances, these circumstances were far from normal.

They crept silently past Doctor Doom's office and made their way to the warehouse grounds where Zach had disappeared. They could already hear the pack howling in the distance. Brad shivered.

"Believe me, buddy, we are going to get that blue-haired boy of yours back," Harlan said.

"Promise me you'll be careful. This is one time your lasso won't do you much good. These boys are like wild animals. They can tear you apart."

They crept up to the warehouse and peered through an open door where a dozen figures gyrated in the light of a bonfire, their muscles glistening. While they looked to be exquisite specimens of manhood, their animal-like cries were unnerving.

"Wow, what beauties! Those boys could make a killing as strippers," Harlan noted with approval.

"Uh, yeah," Brad said. "Probably better if they don't do any more killing of any sort, though."

Harlan nearly let out a guffaw. Brad shushed him just in time by putting a finger to his lip. They crept off to the far side of the pier. Brad wanted Harlan well away from the gathering before he entered the building. He needed his mind to be clear instead of worrying about other things.

He was just about to give the go-ahead when footsteps approached. They froze and hugged the shadows. A figure appeared out of the darkness. It was one of the wild boys. They watched as he stopped and sniffed the air, as though scenting their presence.

Harlan nudged Brad and nodded to the rope tied at his waist. The stripper removed it slowly, coiling it in his hands. This was exactly what Brad had feared. He didn't want Harlan getting involved in anything physical. While Brad had witnessed the superhuman strength of these creatures, Harlan wasn't prepared for how they would fight back or their complete lack of inhibition when it came to killing.

The figure took one step closer to their hiding place. Brad felt Harlan tense in preparation to go on the attack. If that happened, he didn't know what he'd do. Without warning, a hare bolted right in front of them. The boy leapt on it, tearing it apart with his teeth and fingers.

Harlan's jaw dropped. Neither of them moved until the boy had eaten his fill and moved off again.

"Holy shit, Red! What was that thing?" Harlan hissed.

"That thing is what we need to avoid if we want to get out of this alive. And there are plenty of others around."

"Okay," Harlan said. "Let's get this sucker on the road."

They checked the area surrounding the pier. The coast was clear.

Once Harlan was set up, Brad turned back to the warehouse. Judging by the sounds from inside, it looked as though the gang had taken over the building for the night. Or maybe this was their permanent home. Who could say? If so, they had a good stronghold at their disposal, one that was large enough to house a small community of marauding killers.

He entered downwind, taking up a position just inside the main entrance but well out of the light. He searched for signs of Zach. While he could be anywhere, it made sense that he'd be near the pack if they had taken him. *The one you seek is alive*, Madame Leah had said. It might be a slim hope, but it was worth hanging onto when all hope seemed lost. Still, Brad couldn't shake the warning that followed: *Beware when you met him again*.

Whatever was going on down by the river defied logic. From what he'd seen, these boys weren't quite human, though they looked human except for a slight blue tinge under the skin. Other than that, there was nothing to tip you off that they might be in any way abnormal until you witnessed their reptilian strength and agility.

Brad looked up. Clouds obscured the moon. A storm was brewing. All his senses were alert as he felt the heat and humidity on his skin. Up ahead, a sentry who had been nodding off abandoned his post in answer to a whistle just as the first few drops splattered on the roof. Taking advantage of the movement, Brad slipped into the shadow of an oversized coil of rope.

He watched as one of the boys bent and picked up a pair of sticks before flinging a trash can lid through the open space. A second boy jumped up and caught it. The pair sent a frenzied beat crashing through the air as they pounded on the can and the lid.

Others took up the rhythm, clapping hands and shuffling feet. Their cries filled the air. It began to dawn on Brad what those sticks were: bones. And they were long enough to be of the human variety. Just then, a drop of sweat rolled from his brow and inched down his nose, clinging for a moment before falling. He reached out a hand to swipe it away, but missed. The drop fell to the dusty floor where it was absorbed by the dirt.

That could be bad news.

It was exactly the sort of thing these boys seemed to sniff out. He feared what would happen if one of those prowling figures caught his scent.

A trap door jutted up from some nether region

beneath the pier. Now and again, one of the gang descended into its depths before returning moments later with a jubilant cry. Clearly, something was going on below. Brad wondered if that was where they were keeping Zach.

The rain continued to beat a tattoo on the tin roof high overhead. The whoops and cries reached a fever pitch when the trap door opened again and a new figure emerged. As he stepped out, the door slammed shut and the tribe let out a collective howl. It seemed like some sort of initiation ceremony.

The new boy stood before them in a tracksuit and hoodie. Here was yet another exquisite specimen of manhood. Apart from being slightly overdressed, he seemed pretty much like all the others.

A sharp *crack!* resounded from the parking lot. Harlan had just let off the first volley of fireworks.

Now it begins, Brad thought.

The dancers turned toward the sound. Brad hoped Harlan was well away by now. As one, the tribe was off and running toward the parking lot. All but the new figure, who seemed unsure of himself and unsteady on his feet. Eventually he too left, following the others.

Brad dashed to the trap and tugged on the latch. It finally opened with considerable effort. He descended the steps to a dark, narrow corridor beneath the warehouse. Using his penlight, he followed the passage to a thick wooden door.

Inside, the walls gleamed with a blue-white light. Brad glanced over a bewildering array of long metal tables and blinking machines. It looked like a mortuary.

He quickly skirted the space, searching for hidden doors or access routes. Time was running out. He stuck his head inside a standing metal cabinet, a make-shift shower with many dangling showerheads. Something resembling the discarded skin of a large snake lay tangled on the floor. A set of watery footsteps led away from it.

Brad took one last look around before heading back upstairs. Tension hung in the air. The bonfire still burned at the centre of the warehouse. The fireworks continued to explode outside, accompanied by the startled yips and yelps of the tribe. Brad slipped across the empty space, into the shadow of the giant coil. Just then he heard a distinctive slither, like footsteps gliding over a slippery surface accompanied by grunting, as though something heavy were being lifted by brute force.

Brad leapt aside just as the coil landed with a thud that reverberated through the warehouse. A sudden flare from the bonfire showed Brad he wasn't alone. The new boy had returned. And while he may have been slow moving, he was certainly strong.

As the two stood facing one another in the dark, Brad listened to the boy's quiet breathing. He was well aware that these creatures were formidable. The prospect of hand-to-hand combat with one of them offered what would almost inevitably be a losing proposition.

Overhead, a heavy metal hook glinted in the

233

firelight. It might just be possible to grab it and swing out of range, Brad thought. But then what?

The new boy let out a howl as he approached Brad like an animal circling its prey. His eyes gleamed. Without warning, he lunged.

Clammy hands gripped Brad's throat. Instinctively, he grabbed for the hook. For a moment, his fingers grasped empty air. Then suddenly they connected and he smashed the hook into his attacker's skull. An inhuman scream sprang from the boy as he went limp and fell to the floor. The body twitched for five, ten, fifteen seconds, before it finally stopped and lay there unmoving.

Brad knelt and put a finger to the boy's jugular. There was no pulse. He'd broken his neck. If he hadn't connected the first time it would have been him lying there dead right now.

"I'm sorry, pal, but it was you or me," he said, pulling the hoodie from the boy's head.

Blue hair tumbled from underneath the garment. Brad gasped as he stared down at Zach's lifeless face.

"Please no!"

Shouts came from outside in the parking lot. As Brad lifted his head, he heard whistles. A shot went off, followed by a second. The police had arrived.

Brad looked down at the figure sprawled at his feet. A Roman numeral "I" had been tattooed in the curve between Zach's neck and shoulder, that space where Brad had loved to plant kisses every morning when they woke and last thing at night before they went to sleep.

When had Zach got a tattoo?

Before he could think, Bradford found himself surrounded by New Orleans's finest. His arms were wrenched roughly behind his back and cuffed. There was no subtlety in the grip or in the officer's intent. Any man in worse physical shape than Brad might have found his shoulder dislocated or his arms broken.

"Do not try to resist. Ya'll are under arrest for murder."

22

The officer who unlocked Brad's cell the next morning gave him a look that was a mixture of awe and disgust. His cap was pulled well down over his forehead, but Brad could still read his expression loud and clear.

"I don't know what strings y'all pulled to get yerself released," he said, "but I was told to let you out of here and keep my mouth shut. What are y'all supposed to be, anyway? The president's boyfriend or something?"

Brad attempted a smile. Good old Grace was having him sprung. "Don't tell anyone, but the president and his wife are into threesomes."

The officer led Brad down the hall to claim his belongings.

"I never once't before had to let a murderer off the hook so easily," he said, shaking his head.

He waited while Brad signed a release sheet for his possessions.

"Then again," the man said with a sidelong glance. "I'm not so sure y'all did kill anybody last night. Since when doesn't a corpse bleed?"

With that cryptic comment, he left and closed

the door behind him.

Brad pocketed his wallet and cell phone, grateful that for once they'd been spared. He stepped out into the morning sunlight and headed back to the Lion's Roar.

Quint approached the gates on Brad's return. He stopped dead at the property line and stood looking out with grave concern.

"Take care!" he cried, his usual refrain.

Brad stared at the "V" tattooed in the soft space between Quint's neck and shoulder. Funny he hadn't made the connection before.

"Take care of what, Quint? What is it you're so worried about?"

Quint shook his head and looked balefully around. "Ah cain't leave the garden!"

"Why can't you leave the garden?"

"Devils will eat Quint's soul," he said, shivering in the morning sunlight.

"Who told you that, Quint?" Brad demanded. "Who told you devils would eat your soul? Was it the Reverend Septimus Morgenstern of the Tabernacle of the True Vine?"

Quint shook his head. "No."

"Then who was it?"

Quint stared at him. "Dog."

"Who is Dog?"

"Dog looks after us all. We are all his children."

"And Dog said that devils would eat your soul if you left the garden?"

Quint nodded vigorously. Tears formed in his eyes and fell to the ground.

Brad softened his voice. The boy was terrified. If he was going to get anything out of him, it would be through kindness, not bullying or anger.

"What is a soul, Quint? Do you know what a soul is?"

Quint rubbed a tear from his eyes. After a moment, he shook his head. "No, ah don't know."

"Neither do I," Brad told him. "Neither does anybody else, but I have an idea what it might be."

He waited as the boy looked at him with questioning eyes.

"Do you want to hear what I think?"

Quint nodded slightly.

"I think a soul is the unseen part of us that is inside everyone. And because it can't be seen, it can't be harmed. No devil can eat your soul. It's an inner drive that gives our lives meaning and purpose. It's what brings us joy and makes us feel alive. If you can feel those things then your soul is safe and happy. It's always with you and no one can take it away from you. It's what makes us who we are."

Quint was smiling now. "Like love?"

"Yes," Brad said. "It's a lot like love. We can feel it even if we can't see it. But no one can take it away from us, no matter how they hurt us or try to harm the people we love."

"Ah love Derek and Philip," Quint said simply.

"And they love you."

"For always?"

Brad cocked his head. He'd come this far. What to tell this boy that wouldn't send him reeling backward now into fear?

"I think maybe love is eternal, too," he said at last. "Like the soul."

Quint was watching him intently.

"I think it's what survives of us long after we're gone."

"Ah hope so," Quint replied.

Brad's hand strayed to the boy's neck and gave it a gentle caress. His flesh felt cool to the touch. The bluish tinge lay just beneath the skin, visible now in the bright sunlight. "What can you tell me about this tattoo on your neck, Quint?"

Quint reached up and grasped Bard's hand. "No one ever touched me there before."

"Did you have it done or did someone do it for you?" Brad asked.

"Ah had it when ah was begun," he said.

Bradford gave him a long hard look. "How old are you Quint?"

"Last week ah was nineteen. This week ah'm twenty."

"Another birthday," Brad said, as understanding began to grow. He recalled the Gumbos, I through IV, each living one month successively longer than its predecessor. Twenty weeks makes five months, he thought to himself. So I'm guessing that is your allotted span.

Quint turned and looked at him. "Mr. Bradford, do ah have a soul?"

"Yes, you do, Quint," Brad said. "Everybody does. Good people and even bad people. We all have a soul."

"Like love," Quint said. He looked disconsolately to the garden. "But things end."

239

"Yes," Brad agreed, recalling the burial ground behind the pond at the back of the property. "Everything you can see comes to an end. Like our bodies, for instance. We all end sometime. Even the world will end one day. But maybe not love. Maybe love—like the soul—lasts forever."

"Ah'm going to end," Quint said quietly. Another tear rolled down his face. "Any day now."

After a long while, Brad said, "Yes, Quint. I think you are going to end." He waited, but Quint continued to stare at the ground. "Were there other boys named Quint in the garden or at least other boys who looked like you?"

Quint stared directly into the sun, his eyes unflinching. "There was Uno. He looked just like me."

"What happened to Uno?"

"He ended."

"Did you bury him?"

He nodded.

"And was there a Dewey who looked like you?"

"Yes," he said softly. "He ended too. And so did Trey and Quatro. They all ended. Now it's Quint's turn."

"Is that why you left the garden, Quint? Because you didn't want to end?"

Quint nodded.

"Quint, can you tell me the first thing you remember from the very first day you recall anything about your life?"

"Ah lived in the garden with the others," Quint said simply. "Ah lived there and watched the big yellow—ah mean, the *sun*—go up and go down. It

240

was happy there. *Ah* was happy."

"And then what happened?"

"Dog said, 'Don't leave the garden.'"

"And what did you say, Quint?"

"Ah said, 'All right, Dog. Quint won't leave.'"

"But you did leave, didn't you?"

Quint shuddered. "Ah didn't mean to, but Gumbo ran out of the gate and ah went to get him. A car hit him and he ended. Ah had to bring him back and bury him before the devils ate his soul."

Brave boy, Brad thought. In my book, that buys you a membership to the Club of the Human Condition. If you really want in, that is. "And that was when you realized you could leave the garden if you chose to. But the devils came after you, didn't they?"

Tears splashed freely onto Quint's bare feet. "Yes," he whispered. "They wanted to end me. They wanted to eat my soul. Dog says so."

Brad put a hand on the boy's shoulder. "Dog is wrong. The devils can't eat your soul because your soul lives forever, Quint. Remember I told you that?"

Quint looked up and smiled. "Yes, Mr. Bradford. Ah remember."

"What happened after you left the garden, Quint? Can you tell me?"

The boy raised his hands defensively. "Take care!" he cried.

"It's all right," Brad said. "Just tell me what happened."

"Devils chased me down the streets. Ah ran and ran. Ah was faster than them, but they were

241

smarter and some of them ran down another street. Quint didn't know there could be so many streets in the big, wide world. It's too big, Mr. Bradford. When ah came out at the far end they were waiting. They hurt Quint. They tried to end him."

"But they didn't end you. You're still here, aren't you?"

"Surely."

"And is that when you ran up to the inn and knocked on the door?"

"Ah don't remember," he said.

"But you made it here and Derek and Philip have been very good to you. Did they let you in, Quint?"

More tears fell. Quint nodded. "Derek and Philip looked after Quint."

The boy was shaking with fear, but Brad knew he had to press him. They were so close now. "Can you remember where the garden is, Quint?"

Quint shot him a terrified look. "Please," he whimpered. "Ah don't want to remember. Cain't leave the garden!"

"But you can, Quint. You can leave the garden. You *did* leave the garden."

Quint nodded, but his eyes wouldn't meet Bradford's. "Afraid," he said at last.

"I understand," Brad said. "But this may be the only chance I have to find out what happened to Zach. I love Zach, Quint, and I need to find him. If you take me there, I will do everything not to let anyone hurt you. Will you help me?"

Quint nodded. "All right, Mr. Bradford."

He reached out and touched Brad's hand. His fingers seemed only a little bit cold now that the sun had warmed them.

23

Brad followed Quint down Dauphine Street and across the tracks where the warehouses began, past the derelict disco with its inspirational slogans and the giant, perfect torso of a dancing boy towering over the landscape.

Quint shook uncontrollably as they headed deeper into Bywater, but he didn't turn back. Brad had only an inkling of what might be going through his head and where he was taking them when suddenly he stopped dead. From across the field, Brad saw Doctor Doom's forbidding hand with its fancy digits: Cadillac, Disneyland, Amazon, Monopoly, and Microsoft World. The coolant car gleamed in the distance.

Quint looked about fearfully. "Dog lives here."

Brad nodded. "Thank you for bringing me here. I won't make you go any further, Quint. Is this where you grew up?"

"Yes. Quint begun here. Quint was very bad for leaving." He looked around nervously. "No devils yet. But they surely will come."

"They're not devils, Quint, but they will come. You can go back now."

Quint looked fearfully as Brad turned to go.

"Take care!" he cried.

"I'll be all right, Quint. I promise you." He waved as though they were old friends bidding one another farewell.

"So long, Mr. Bradford," Quint said. "Ah love you."

"And I love you, Quint. You are a very good and brave person. Thank you for bringing me here. Everything's going to be fine now."

In the distance, someone had spray-painted across one of the walls: *Why are you always following me?* An apt question, Brad thought.

"It's all coochie hoochie, Mr. Bradford," he heard Quint say from behind him.

Brad smiled. "Isn't it, though?"

He headed for the caretaker's officer then stopped dead and slowly looked back at Quint's retreating form.

"It's all coochie hoochie, Derek," Quint had said.

"You mean hoochie coochie, Quint," Derek had answered.

"Dog looks after his own," Quint had said.

"I think you mean 'God.' God looks after His own,'" Brad had replied.

"Take care! Take care!" It was Quint's constant refrain. Brad smacked his forehead. Of course! How could he have been so stupid? Quint hadn't been cautioning them at all, but rather warning them. Not "Take care!" but "Caretaker!"

Brad felt a shiver run down his spine. He looked up and saw in the distance the icy cool lozenge of the refrigerant car gleaming eerily in the sun. He knew now who had been behind the kidnappings and the murders. Not Dog, not even some malevolent God, but a simple caretaker.

He crept quietly through the fence and made his way into the field where the sign read, "Garden." Yes, he really should have known.

Everything looked the same as before, with one single exception: there was now another bump of dirt in the line of graves. Someone or something had been interred. He hoped it was merely Gumbo IV and not Zachary I.

Brad looked warily around. He also hoped Gumbo V hadn't yet had time to develop into a full-fledged, hyper-watchdog along the lines of its predecessor. There was no sign of a new prototype. He'd take that as good news, but clutched his *gris-gris* just in case.

Brad turned a corner of the building and almost cried for joy. There was Harlan, walking side by side with another boy. But wait! What was Harlan doing here? He slipped into the shadows in time to hear Harlan say, "Dog says we have to make sure no one else gets into the garden."

"'Dog says'?" Brad thought. *Oh-oh.*

Just then he felt the tip of a Taser prodding the nape of his neck.

"Beautiful, aren't they?" came the whiney little voice from the whiney little man at his side. "I c-c-created them in my image."

Brad put his hands behind his head. "Doctor Doom, I presume? Or should I say, 'God'?"

The caretaker grinned. "My l-l-little joke," he said with a grin. "Some days I feel just like M-M-Marlon Brando in *The Island of Doctor Moreau.*"

"Must be a great ego boost," Brad said.

"Ah, another judgemental type. Well, you can't p-p-please everyone."

"What exactly did you hope to accomplish here?"

The caretaker shrugged. "To sh-sh-shine a light on the inexplicable darkness of the universe, to bring f-f-fire down from the heavens and give it to the heathens. That s-s-sort of thing. I also thought maybe l-l-life everlasting on earth rather than in Heaven might be a good perk."

"Is that why you brought them up to be killers?" Brad asked.

"Not all of them are k-k-killers. They are created neither good nor evil. But they c-c-can be programmed to choose."

"To choose to do your bidding."

He felt the Taser poke him. "Or yours. Or anyone's really. Why not? I created them. Why sh-sh-shouldn't they do what I want them to do? You'll make a very f-f-fine model yourself. I think I'll m-m-make you a Sexual Favours version, with off-time duties as f-f-floor mopper and toilet scrubber."

"I'm kind of that now," Brad said, slowly turning to face his captor. "Particularly the latter. But I'm flattered you think I'm perfect enough to bother reproducing."

"Not quite, but I can weed out some of the im-p-p-perfections."

"There was a guy named Hitler who thought like you."

The caretaker scowled. "You know what your problem is?"

"Bad table manners?"

"N-n-no, you don't learn from your mistakes."

"Ah—you've been talking to my boss."

"Right this way please," the little man said, nudging him along the path ahead. "By the way, how is Quint? He's one of m-m-my little miracles. He was the first five-monther I created. I'd l-l-like to see him again before he ends in"—here he looked at his watch—"about four hours from now."

Brad shook his head. He'd been right in his timeline calculations, unfortunately for Quint.

"Am I to understand you've perfected some kind of zombie-making process or is this particular achievement more in the 'clone' category?"

"Oh, never zombies! Nothing so primitive." The little man looked at him shrewdly. "What you're r-r-really asking is whether the original humans used as prototypes for my experiments are still alive. The answer is, largely, yes. They're in a s-s-state of organic suspension. Something like cryogenics, but reversible." He looked off briefly to the coolant car. "I had a f-f-few early failures. They were heartbreaking, to say the l-l-least. As for the rest, well—suffice to say that you can't copy energy, you can only b-b-borrow it. Or steal it. I won't b-b-bore you with my theories of sub-atomic particle regeneration. Once I've perfected the c-c-copies, I'll have to eliminate the originals."

"You make copies of people and kill the originals? What's the point? Why not just stick with the originals?"

"That's the only way I'll be able to make sure they last forever." He sighed. "You wouldn't understand."

Brad rolled his eyes. "Oh, right. And you think *you're* misunderstood."

They had reached the warehouse. The little man motioned Brad toward the trap door with his Taser. Brad opened it and headed down, hands behind his head.

"And what about Hedy? Why did you kill her?"

"Technically, I didn't. I sent one of my b-b-boys to do it when she threatened t-t-to expose my operations. She thought he was there to accept her offer of half a million dollars to l-l-let homeless people come and live here with Doctor Doom. Imagine, all those imperfect p-p-people running around with my perfect creations. It would have been ghastly."

"She wanted to create a refugee camp down here."

"Exactly! And where I was creating a p-p-paradise on earth, she was trying to bring her little band of refugees and misfits in to repopulate things."

"And the incriminating letters from her husband?"

"I have them. In case I need p-protection."

They reached the room where Brad had searched for Zach the night before. He'd obviously been close. The little man pressed a button and a panel slid open revealing a room full of giant cylinders, each containing test-tube humans.

Brad's breath was coming out in wisps.

"Temperature control," said the little man. "It's a c-c-crucial part of the operation. We need to be very careful in here. One f-f-false move and we'd both be dead. " He giggled. "Absolute zero k-k-kills anything."

At the far end of the room, Brad saw a console

covered in blinking lights. There was still no sign of Zach.

"Ah, you're admiring my c-c-control room. Shatter-proof glass. That's where everything ha-ha-happens. But don't think of getting in there and stopping things. Anyone who trips the switch in the control room to release the capsules in here will be instantly f-f-frozen. It's such a delicate balance."

"This could be a great scientific discovery," Brad said. "You could be famous."

"Famously dead. Don't g-g-give me that crap. They'd kill me and b-b-bury what I've done in seconds." He sighed. "Sorry. This is g-g-going to hurt a bit."

The little man raised the Taser. Brad felt the beginnings of an earthquake rumbling through his nervous system as he passed out cold.

He was back in the City of the Dead. A chill wind blew by. Somewhere a train went past, shaking the ground beneath his feet. Brad found himself looking around like a tourist scouring a T-shirt shop for that perfect message to convey his innermost feelings to show just how unique he really was. But in fact there was no message to express how he felt or show what made him different from all the other petrified figures in the City of the Dead. Another train rumbled by, this one a little closer. Brad ignored it and concentrated on his surroundings. He reminded himself he wasn't so different after all. Down there he was just one more stiff among thousands—hell, billions! What on earth had ever convinced him he was in any way special?

A final train went by and the rumbling stopped.

But his body kept shivering. In fact, he was freezing!

When he came to, Brad found himself strapped to a table. He was unable to move his arms and legs. At best, he could just turn his head from side to side. He was surrounded by dozens of tables, each with a body strapped to it. The bodies appeared to be alive, though they all had tubes and wires attaching them to various machines. These were the real humans, he realized. The figures behind glass were the creations. He craned his head, but try as he might he couldn't see Zach or Harlan.

His breath came out in white flags. The chill he'd experienced in his dream was real. Brad's nostrils caught a whiff of smoke. It was an acrid, chemical smell. It worried him. Was Doctor Doom mad enough to burn down his own laboratories to ensure that no one learned his secret?

Yes, he probably was. In fact, Brad wondered, was any part of the man even remotely sane? He raised his head and looked around at the frozen zombie figurines in the glass cylinders and the real humans strapped to tables. This wasn't a City of the Dead so much as burial ground for the living.

Brad heard footsteps. The little man suddenly appeared, Taser in hand, and stood looking down on Brad.

"Who else have you created?" Brad asked, recalling the James Dean and Montgomery Clift look-a-likes. "Marilyn?"

"Yes."

"JFK?"

"Oh, yes!"

"Elvis?""

The caretaker sneered. "I don't do Elvis."

"Where are the rest of your victims?"

"Not victims!" He looked aghast. "Guests! Like your blue-haired friend, Mr. Kong. He was so brave trying to rescue you. That's the only r-r-reason you're still here. I preferred him to you, and I had only room for o-o-one that evening." He frowned. "They're all still alive and breathing now, but I'll have to k-k-kill them, of course. A little fire will do the trick. By the time the firemen g-g-get there, there won't be much left. They won't f-f-find much—just a few burned corpses. Even if they bother to trace them, they'll s-s-simply turn out to be people who went m-m-missing after Katrina."

"Why are you doing this?"

"It's God's handiwork. I'm just lending a helping h-h-hand. It's in the Bible, isn't it? Something about throwing the heathens out of Paradise. Or wait—is that the Bhagavad-Gita? Not that I care. I'm a scientist."

"You could team up with some politicians I know," Brad said. "Isn't that what they all want? All the dictators and great despots? No sharing of Paradise."

The little man frowned and set his Taser on the edge of a table. "Spoil sport. I c-c-certainly won't resuscitate you."

He walked over to a cabinet, extracting a long white gown then pulling on a pair of surgical gloves before stepping over to a tray of medical implements. Brad watched as he picked up a long tube and carried it back to the table with him. He dreaded to think where that might end up.

"If you don't struggle, this won't hurt too much," said the little man.

The tube was inserted in Brad's right nostrils and taped down.

"The anaesthetic n-n-needs to be a constant drip, otherwise t-t-terrible things can happen."

The little man ambled over to a fat cylinder and turned the tap.

"Betcha can't c-c-count to a hundred," he said with a laugh.

He had just gone over to a wall unit and picked up the ends of three coloured wires when his expression registered an alert. Brad glanced across the room to where Quint stood in the doorway.

"Let Mr. Bradford go," Quint said to the doctor. "Or ah will end you, Dog."

"You still have that little speech quirk, I see. A small p-p-problem with the left frontal lobe." The little man turned and addressed Bradford. "It does some f-f-funny things to them, now and again. Sometimes they reverse words, other times they speak foreign languages."

He turned back to Quint. "I'm so glad to see you again, Quint. Your time is running out, I'm afraid. I can fix it for you if you do what I say."

Quint's eyes glinted with purpose. "No, Dog. It's Quint's turn to end. Let Mr. Bradford go."

The doctor eyed the Taser he'd left on the table ten feet away. "That wouldn't be w-w-wise. If you end now, there will be no one to b-b-bury you. If no one buries you, the devils will eat your soul and you will be in eternal torment."

"No one can eat mah soul, Dog, because they cain't see it. An' because ah love Mr. Bradford and Philip and Derek."

The boy began to sniffle.

"Poor Quint," said the doctor. "You've discovered the t-t-truth of being human: love hurts."

Quint looked up angrily. "You untie Mr. Bradford or ah will end you with mah bare hands."

He made a move toward the doctor. The little man started.

"Okay, Quint," he said. "I will untie him. Stay c-c-calm."

The doctor unlaced Bradford's hands. As Brad sat up and massaged the stiffness from his wrists, the doctor lunged for the Taser. He reached it a second before Quint and jabbed the boy in the side. Quint's body shuddered and fell to the floor.

"The w-w-wonders of science," the doctor said with a smirk.

He turned back to Brad, but Quint revived more quickly than the doctor anticipated. With a single blow, the boy sent the doctor flying across the room. The little man got to his feet and, looking fearfully about, dashed into the control room and locked the door behind him.

Quint followed, pounding on the shatter-proof glass. It wobbled, but did not break.

Brad scrabbled to untie his feet. He had just got free when he looked up in time to see Quint wrench the control room door from its frame, sending a shower of broken glass into the laboratory. The doctor cowered inside the booth.

"No!" he screamed.

Quint hurled himself at the little man, sending them both flying into one of the upright cylinders. Brad watched in horror as it smashed and the contents came splashing down, freezing them both instantly.

"Oh, Quint," Brad said softly, gazing at the boy's frozen body.

Half a mile down the waterfront, sirens wailed. With lights flashing, a convoy of emergency vehicles arrived on the scene. A long plume of greasy smoke rose in the air. A pier was on fire. This was the noxious chemical smell that had Brad worried when he woke and found himself strapped to a table.

Brad clutched Zach tightly, as they watched police officers swarming over the pier. His lover's skin was still cold and he was shivering violently, but he seemed otherwise unharmed.

"Th-th-thanks for rescuing us," Zach said.

A stutter! Frightening thoughts passed through Brad's mind. He glanced down at the nape of Zach's neck. Thank god, he thought: there was no tattoo. It was just a chill then. This was the real deal.

Brad hailed Harlan and the Japanese couple as they staggered out of the smoke toward him. He waited hopefully, but there was no sign of a Quint look-a-like. No Chester Morgenstern.

A cop stood to one side watching the scenario. As they carried Quint's frozen body out of the lab, he looked down in disgust and nodded to a subordinate: "Y'all get someone down here to get rid of this Mr. Freezie Pop."

Bradford turned to the cop. "Have some respect," he said. "That was a human being once."

24

When Bradford woke the next morning, the tube sticking out of his arm made him think he was back in Doctor Doom's laboratory. Then he remembered Quint and how the boy had sacrificed himself to save Brad and Zach and all the others. Whatever Quint was, for whatever purpose he may have been created, he had had the noblest of human aspirations. And I, Bradford thought, must have had some awfully good luck to still be alive. He looked down at the *gris-gris* tied around his neck. Madame Leah had told him to hold tight to his beliefs. It seemed to be working.

Zach beamed at him from across the hospital room. His skin had lost its bluish tinge and his temperature had returned to normal. There seemed to be no lingering after-effects of whatever state he'd been kept in the entire time he'd been missing. It was good to have things return to normal.

"They weren't really zombies," Zach was saying of the doctor's creations. "But they weren't quite clones either. The ones with higher consciousness levels were close to being human.

From what I could tell, it was some sort of energy transfer that made it work. I can even dimly remember some of the things that happened to my alternate being in the short time he was alive."

He looked at Brad.

"Uh, yeah ... about that knock on the head," Brad began.

"I actually remember that hook you swung at me."

"Right."

"Don't worry. I don't hold it against you. Given the chance, I probably would have killed you too."

Brad's mouth hung open.

"It's as though my alternate's memories have become mine, what little there were of them, now that I've got all my energy back."

"So it was like an exchange of consciousness?" Brad asked. "Kind of like your belief in reincarnation, how one thing becomes another but stays essentially the same inside?"

Zach cocked his head. "It's a little like that, but the correct word would be 'transference' rather than 'reincarnation'. In any event, the copies had some sort of psychic link with their living counter parts, but through a dormant mind."

"I still don't understand why they took you and not me the night you were kidnapped."

Zach looked a little sheepish. He said, "The doctor explained that before he put me under. He said you were too old."

Brad's face fell.

"Sorry. He only wanted boys in their twenties. By thirty, he said, the chromosome degeneration

257

process has set in."

Brad harrumphed. "He told me it was because he had only room for one that night."

"He was probably just going to kill you instead of clone you." Zach shrugged. "Anyway, that's why he chose me instead of you."

Brad looked over at a beautiful bunch of white chrysanthemums. "Thanks for the flowers, by the way."

"Actually," Zach said, "they're from Harlan. He wants us to visit him in Indiana. I've got the address of his ranch. I told him we'd get there one day."

Brad's phone buzzed. It was Grace. She'd already been apprised of the goings on, including the fact that Hedy had been killed because she tried to buy the property where Doctor Doom had his laboratory. What she told Brad next, however, was a big surprise: the shaved-headed man had actually been working with the FBI to determine what sort of unusual cloning was happening down there.

"He wasn't a realtor?" Brad exclaimed.

"Not at all. But don't feel sorry for him. Once they took over the property they were going to force the little man to reveal his secret formula and use it for themselves."

"That's an entirely frightening prospect," Brad said.

"I agree wholeheartedly, Red. Fortunately for the world—or perhaps unfortunately, depending on your perspective—the doctor never wrote down his procedures. He kept everything in his head, so we'll never know if there was a recipe for perfecting life."

258

"Probably for the best."

"That would be my take. I gather the good doctor had been on the FBI's radar for some time, but until recently he'd been flying a little too low for them to pick him up. Hedy's murder tipped them off that things were moving ahead quickly."

"As much of a monster as he was, I think he was the victim of his own warped mind."

"Yes, he was that most unfortunate of human beings..." Grace began.

"An overweight gay man?"

"Worse, a thwarted genius."

"We could quibble over that," Brad said.

"You'll be glad to know that Hedy's husband, the redoubtable Tyrone Pritchard, is currently being investigated for fraud and bribery. The FBI again." Grace's tone was nonchalant. "Not that anything will come of it down there. They seem to have a rather peculiar concept of justice in those southern states." She *tsked*. "And life goes on."

For some of us, anyway, Brad thought.

"Oh, by the way—there's one piece of good news," Grace said. "I heard through the grapevine that the money Hedy wanted to use to build housing for the homeless might actually get used for that purpose. Apparently it's a question of ownership."

"But I thought she stole it," Brad piped up.

"So it would seem. But the tricky part is that if anyone else claims it—her former-boss or her husband, for instance—they would end up in jail because it was unaccounted for in the first place. As far as the rest of the world is concerned, it's 'found' money. I understand Hedy already made clear what

259

she wanted to do with it. I think someone will see their way to making that happen." She paused. "As long as the contents of a certain laptop disappear."

"Funny, I don't recall any laptop other than the one the police already have in their possession," Brad said.

"Let's hope it stays that way."

She clicked off.

"That *is* good news," Zach agreed, when Brad relayed the gist of the conversation. "Maybe one day Hedy Pritchard will become a N'Orleans legend, like Marie Laveau, as someone who dedicated herself to helping the sick and the poor."

"It would make a great story."

An hour later, Brad and Zach arrived at the Lion's Roar to find Derek and Philip sitting in the courtyard. Their long faces showed they were still in mourning for Quint.

"This place just won't be the same without him," Philip said, shaking his head.

"You might try to locate Quint's successor. I understand the doctor was trying to make longer-lasting models," Brad told him. "I told you I'm pretty sure I saw a new model wandering around New Orleans twice in the past week."

Derek looked off wistfully. "Yes," he said. "We might. But he wouldn't be the same, would he?"

Brad nodded sadly. "Probably not. Whatever he was, Quint wasn't a robot."

"Anything but," Derek added. "We'll miss him."

A loud *miaow* sounded. Brad looked over to see a white cat, tail erect and with a crook at the end, parading past the pool.

"Well, somebody's happy," Brad said.

"Derek and ah will adopt her, if no one claims her," Philip said. "The dogs like her, so she won't be a problem."

"Any news of Gerald?"

"He'll be all right," Philip said. "Though ah think it will take him a long time to get over Hedy."

"And the police are convinced he's innocent?" Zach asked.

"Apparently the fingerprints on the murder weapon are a match for someone who went missing in Katrina. Ah guess we'll just have to let the police figure that one out."

"How are the Japanese boys?" Brad asked.

"Recovering from their ordeal," Derek said. He winked. "I gather they've got a whole lot of footage for their documentary about some bees."

"Can't wait to see it," Brad said. "Call us if they hold the premiere here."

Mounting their bicycles, Brad and Zach headed to the river and stood looking out over the water. The Mississippi was a mighty snake wending its way up and down the coast. New Orleans, that most colourful and eccentric of cities, was just one of its many ports of call along the way.

"Despite everything, I hate to leave," Zach said. "But we're pretty much done here."

"I agree. What they do with the rebuilding is up to the people who return." Which leaves just one last stop, Brad thought. "I've got a debt to pay before we go. Care for a little side trip to the City of the Dead?"

"You lead. I'll follow."

They turned their bicycles in at the cemetery gate and wheeled down to the mausoleum bearing the name of New Orleans's famed Voodoo queen. As usual, a gaggle of gullible tourists stood around listening to the patter of a beaming tour guide. Only this one seemed to get the legend right, explaining how people asked Marie's favour then marked an X on the tomb, followed by a second X marking the vision that told of its acknowledgement. A third X, he said, indicated that the wish had come true.

Without waiting for the group to move on, Brad walked up to the tomb and picked up a piece of orange brick. With the group staring at him, he located his first two X's then marked a third one at the end of the series. He dropped a few more silver coins in the cup at the base of the mausoleum.

"Debt paid," he said to the group then left with their eyes boring holes in his back.

As they passed through the cemetery gate something made Brad turn back for a last look. The sun was in his eyes, but he could have sworn he saw a woman in a yellow sun dress who looked very much like Hedy standing next to Marie Laveau's tomb. He watched as she inscribed an X on the side of the edifice, tossed the stone aside and waved to him once before turning away.

"Hey, wait!" Brad yelled, leaving Zach standing bewildered as he ran back.

By the time he reached the tomb the woman had vanished. Brad ran up and down the rows but, try as he might, he couldn't see her anywhere.

"Eyes playing tricks on you?" Zach asked when he returned and told him what he'd seen.

"Maybe," Brad said, shaking his head.

"Don't worry—we'll get you a nice new pair of glasses when we get home."

"Let's go," Brad told him. "Some things it's better not to figure out."

On their way back to the Lion's Roar, they came across an old, one-legged beggar sitting at the side of the road. He clapped his hands as he sang, *Eh, maman! Eh, maman! Les haricots sont pas salés*. His plaintive voice was the cry of a lonesome animal howling in the wilderness. It seemed as if Louisiana had a case of the perpetual blues. Some days, in fact, it almost seemed as if it might last forever. Life was such a dismal, sad affair, Brad thought, remembering Quint.

The singer looked up and saw the sombre expression on Brad's face. "Why is you cryin', friend?" He stretched an arm toward the horizon. "Why, jes lookey here. Why is you cryin' when they is all this glory to be had?"

He offered them up his bottle with a toothless smile. Brad took a swig. It was good, home-grown bourbon. He passed it to Zach. Zach took a drink and went to pass it back to the old man, but the singer nodded to Brad.

"His turn again. He need two swigs. He look like a man destroyed."

Brad took another, wiping his mouth with his hand in true country style before passing it back.

The old man winked. "That's right! *Laissez les bon ton roulet*, friends," he exclaimed. "Even when it's bad, you is still in N'Orleans, yeah? And y'all know that has *got* to be good!"

END

Acknowledgements

Thanks to the inimitable Greg Herren (a true sinner) and Paul Willis (a veritable saint) for inviting me to *Saints and Sinners*. Thanks also to Shane McConnell, boy genius, who was there, to Floyd McLamb and Stuart Anthony for their unmatched hospitality at the Lions Inn in the Faubourg Marigny (Funkytown), to Dan Rodger for guiding me to that little oasis far from home, and to Lynn Krause for the company. I tip my hat to Christian Morgenstern for a certain rabbity verse I would dearly have loved to use here, but wasn't able to. And let's not forget the inimitable Robert Johnston, King of the Delta Blues, and Clifton Chenier, King of Zydeco, for the soul. And, of course, thanks to the remarkable spirit that is New Orleans, the city even Katrina couldn't sink: *Les haricots sont pas salés, mais laissez les bon ton roulet!*

Also in this series:

THE P-TOWN MURDERS

The First Bradford Fairfax Mystery

In a place that's "to die for," no one expects to die for real. So muses undercover agent Bradford Fairfax after an anonymous call reveals that his ex-boyfriend, party boy Ross Pretty, has died from an ecstasy overdose in "the gayest place on earth" — Provincetown, Massachusetts. But as the body of another overdose victim washes up on the shores of P-Town, Brad becomes convinced that Ross's death is no accident, and his intention to bury his former lover suddenly turns into a full-scale investigation. It seems that freewheeling P-Town has a dark side, one full of greed, jealousy, and deadly games.

DEATH IN KEY WEST

The Second Bradford Fairfax Mystery

The rich really are different from you and me. On a New Year's vacation in Key West, the original gay Shangri-La, special agent Bradford Fairfax and his blue-haired boyfriend-cum-sidekick Zach meet James Quentin Ashley Vanderbilt III, an improbable "heiress" to one of the world's biggest fortunes, who is convinced his own father wants him dead. At first they dismiss him as yet another eccentric millionaire, but when an infamous group of drag queens are found poisoned, Brad and Zach are thrust into a search for the truth and soon find themselves embroiled in yet another tantalizing mystery. Join the gay man's James Bond and a host of memorable zanies, as he returns in this madcap follow-up to The P-Town Murders!

VANISHED IN VALLARTA

The Third Bradford Fairfax Mystery

On assignment in the fame Mexican resort town, gay caballero Bradford Fairfax discovers he has far more to worry about than sand fleas and *la turista*. When a sultry diva sends out a distress signal, Brad answers the call. But why won't his boss, the shadowy Grace, tell him why he's really in PV? When a fellow agent gets blown away passing on top-secret information, Brad has no idea where to turn. Suddenly everyone seems unusually suspicious. Or suspiciously unusual. And what's a boy to do when his former partner—a.k.a. Little Wing—returns from the dead looking sexier than any corpse should be allowed to look. With romance and intrigue behind every taco stand, our man Brad proves yet again that things are never what they seem!